BACKWOODS BRAWL

Pushing through, Slocum got to Davy's side. The man fought ineffectively against the two Spiders. One held his legs and the other tried to draw his knife across Davy's throat.

Slocum hauled off and landed a haymaker in the knife-wielder's belly. This caused the other man to release Davy's feet and go for a hidden weapon.

Slocum dived forward. His shoulder rammed into the man's rock-hard gut, driving him back into the crowd that was slowly forming in a ring around the fighters. Slocum and the man went down in a flailing pile, each struggling for dominance. Slocum staggered when a blow struck him on the side of the head. He wasn't even sure if it came from the Spider he fought.

"You're the other one," the Spider said, his pig eyes narrowed and glaring at Slocum. "You saved him back at the Web and now you're tryin' to rescue him again. Yellow Henry wants your balls, and I'm gonna give 'em to him on a silver platter!"

A thick-bladed Bowie knife came from the folds of the man's coat. He advanced with the tip toward Slocum in a way that showed long experience with knife fights.

"Get 'em," came the cry from the crowd. Slocum wasn't sure who was being cheered on. He fixed his eyes on the man's wrist, waiting to see the tendons tense for the killing thrust . . .

DON'T MISS THESE
ALL-ACTION WESTERN SERIES
FROM THE BERKLEY PUBLISHING GROUP

THE GUNSMITH by J. R. Roberts
Clint Adams was a legend among lawmen, outlaws, and ladies. They called him . . . the Gunsmith.

LONGARM by Tabor Evans
The popular long-running series about U.S. Deputy Marshal Long—his life, his loves, his fight for justice.

SLOCUM by Jake Logan
Today's longest-running action Western. John Slocum rides a deadly trail of hot blood and cold steel.

BUSHWHACKERS by B. J. Lanagan
An action-packed series by the creators of Longarm! The rousing adventures of the most brutal gang of cutthroats ever assembled—Quantrill's Raiders.

JAKE LOGAN

SLOCUM AND THE JERSEY LILY

J

JOVE BOOKS, NEW YORK

SLOCUM AND THE JERSEY LILY

A Jove Book / published by arrangement with
the author

PRINTING HISTORY
Jove edition / December 1999

The Penguin Putnam Inc. World Wide Web site address is
http://www.penguinputnam.com

ISBN: 0-515-12706-X

A JOVE BOOK®
Jove Books are published by The Berkley Publishing Group,
a division of Penguin Putnam Inc.,
375 Hudson Street, New York, New York 10014.
JOVE and the "J" design
are trademarks belonging to Penguin Putnam Inc.

PRINTED IN THE UNITED STATES OF AMERICA

10 9 8 7 6 5 4 3 2 1

SLOCUM AND THE
JERSEY LILY

1

"Guilty! Pay the fine or I feed you to my bear, Bob." Punctuating the harsh sentence came a hungry growl from a bear that was chained in a corner of the saloon. The snarls; the ferocious teeth; the sharp, flashing claws; the way the burly brute strained at the rusty chain convinced John Slocum that he had only one choice.

He had to pay the fine levied by Judge Roy Bean.

There was a problem, however. Slocum didn't have two nickels to rub together. Riding along in the dusty, hot desert of west Texas had not been pleasant, but running from a band of Comanche intent on separating him from his scalp had added speed to his escape. It hadn't been his fault that the deal with the Comancheros had turned sour and four of the white men had stolen four wagonloads of buffalo hides from the Indians. Slocum had been willing to deal fair and square with the Comanches.

The Indians didn't much care about intentions. All they saw was how they had been cheated. Since the varmints who had stolen the buffalo robes were long gone, that left Slocum and one other man to endure the Comanches' ire.

His partner was long dead, with more bullet holes in him than a rotted wood fence. Slocum did not intend to follow his friend to the Happy Hunting Grounds.

None of that had been his fault. And it sure wasn't his fault that his horse had pulled up lame on the outskirts of Langtry, Texas, in the jurisdiction of the orneriest judge anywhere.

At the moment, Slocum would rather have faced Hanging Judge Isaac Parker on his worst day. A noose was a cleaner death than being mauled by a savage bear.

"You got the money, son, or you gonna be lunch for Bob?" The judge pushed back his wide-brimmed Mexican sombrero and squinted at Slocum, as if peering into his soul. Bean's gray beard twitched, and storm clouds formed in his sharp eyes. Slocum had heard the stories of Roy Bean and didn't cotton much to being on the receiving end of his justice.

One story he heard related how Bean had come across a corpse, searched it, and found forty dollars and a derringer. Rather than steal the money, he had fined the corpse forty dollars for carrying a concealed weapon. Then he had taken the derringer for his own, too. Slocum could see it poking up out of a vest pocket.

"I don't have the money," Slocum said, squaring his shoulders. He didn't see how he could fight his way out of the Jersey Lily Saloon where the judge held court, but he'd rather die with a bullet in him than have a bear gnaw on his still-rattling bones.

"Nobody here'll say I'm not a fair man. No, siree," Roy Bean said pompously. He hitched up his drawers, trying to get his prodigious gut behind the gun belt he wore. He failed. "Give the man a drink, Charlie," he called to the barkeep.

Slocum knocked back the drink. He wondered what it was supposed to be. Whatever was served here, it had no legal claim to being called whiskey. It burned all the way down and then exploded like a stick of dynamite in his belly.

"I'm a fair man. I gave you a free drink 'fore I fed you to Bob. That's as fair as I can be."

The men holding Slocum grabbed his arms and pushed him toward the snarling bear. He lowered one shoulder and got free, swinging his fist to smash into the other man's chest. The punch landed right over the deputy's heart, sending him to the floor, gasping for breath.

"Hold on, son," barked the judge. "Don't get yer dander up none. I ain't feedin' you to Bob. He done et already today. Don't want him gettin' fat like me." Judge Roy Bean chuckled as he rocked back and bounced his paunch.

Slocum stepped away, considering how hard it would be to bolt through the door and get out of Langtry. The town was nothing much more than a railroad track, a big water tank and the Jersey Lily with its battered sign proclaiming JUSTICE OF THE PEACE . . . LAW WEST OF THE PECOS. But the clownish judge was belied by the men with shotguns at the corners of the saloon. Slocum could never reach the door without getting cut to bloody ribbons.

"You know I don't have any money. Your men searched me."

"Well, you got this here fancy-ass watch," Roy Bean said, holding up Slocum's pocket watch. That watch was his only legacy from his brother Robert, killed during Pickett's Charge. Slocum would wrestle the bear to get that watch back. No two-bit judge was going to take it from him.

The expression on his face spoke louder than words ever could. Bean put the watch down in front of him, picked up a gavel and looked at Slocum again, checking his reaction.

"This here watch means the world to you, don't it?"

Slocum did not answer. Roy Bean could read his expression clearly enough to know.

"This changes things a mite. You be willin' to work off yer fine?"

"How?" From all he had seen, Slocum doubted much work got done around Langtry. It would be the work of a lifetime just to clean up the dusty streets. Repairing the few buildings—or just the saloon where Bean held court—

would take the better part of a year to finish.

"We don't believe in chain gangs around here," Bean said. "Bet we'd have to put shackles on you if I tried to put you to work around Langtry. But what I got in mind's a damn sight easier and worlds more pleasant."

The only thing Slocum could think of that fit that description would be putting a bullet in Judge Roy Bean's fat gut and then riding out of town scot-free.

"What is it?"

"You up for this, son?"

Slocum nodded once, waiting for the worst.

"It's like this, Slocum. Thass yer name, ain't it?" Roy Bean didn't slow down long enough to see Slocum nod. He had a far-off expression now, as if he had lost himself in a pleasant dream. He even sighed like a young girl contemplating her first true love. This put Slocum on guard.

"You see, Slocum, I am a great admirer of the Jersey Lily, Mrs. Lily Langtry herself. Now, I have never had the great honor of meetin' this fine lady, but this is gonna change, thanks be to you."

"What do you mean?"

"You, Slocum, are going to go to New Orleans and fetch her back for a special command performance right here, up on the stage of the Jersey Lily. Imagine," Judge Roy Bean said in his lovesick voice, "the fabled Mrs. Lily Langtry right here in the town named after her on the stage of the dance hall named to honor her."

Slocum had heard of Lily Langtry and knew she was a singer from England. Other than this, he had no knowledge of her.

"How do I find her?"

"She's in New Orleans. Everyone there'll know how to find her. She's famous, son. Damned famous." Bean's tone hardened, and Slocum knew he was traveling in treacherous territory now. One mistake and the judge would throw him to the bear.

"Does she know she's supposed to come here to perform for you?"

"How can she possibly deny such a request?" Roy Bean said. "It's a great honor she simply cannot turn down."

"What if her tour doesn't permit it?" Slocum asked. "It's not fair to deprive others of hearing her, is it?"

"Fetch her here," Bean said hotly. He lifted his gavel and held it over Slocum's watch. The judge's hand shook, as if he found it hard to restrain himself from smashing the time-piece. Then Bean laid down the gavel gently and leaned forward, his hands on the bar. "You got a tongue. Use it to convince her she ought to come here."

"If she's in New Orleans and my horse pulled up lame, it might take me a year or more to walk that far."

This time Judge Roy Bean laughed heartily. "Son, I got money. I got lots of money. I'll see you get to New Orleans in time to fetch her 'fore she goes back to England."

Bean heaved himself up on the planks-over-barrel bar and slid across, landing heavily beside Slocum.

"You need to see what all I done around here so's you'll be able to impress her." Bean reached out and grabbed Slocum by the shoulder, dragging him along with a surprisingly strong grip. Even if he had tried, Slocum could not have escaped. The deputies with their shotguns moved quickly behind him, keeping their judge out of the line of fire.

Slocum squinted in the hot west Texas sun and felt the blast furnace heat pound at him until he wanted to sink down in the shade and pray for night. As they walked down the main street, if a dirt road between a half dozen buildings could be called a street, Slocum felt the moisture being sucked from his body.

"Hot day," observed Bean, adjusting his wide-brimmed sombrero to shade his face. "Then, most are out here. We get some water out of the Rio Grande way o'er yonder.

"I got a part interest in the foot bridge 'cross the river. Put an end to the Fitzsimmons–March fight o'er it a while back. Dime a crossin' don't sound like much, but you'd be surprised how much traffic there is. 'Course I let folks use it for free on holidays."

"On your birthday?" asked Slocum.

For a moment, Bean's face turned cloudy with anger, then he laughed uproariously.

"You got a mouth on you, Slocum. A sense of humor, too. I like that. Be glad I like that. I spent most of my life kickin' around out West, and it's made me purty settled in my ways of thinkin'. I was a mule skinner; I run a store. Hell, I even owned my whole damned town outside San Antone."

"Beanville?" Slocum asked. "Heard tell of it. Tough town."

"Tough, but there was law. I saw to that. Left there and moved my family up to Vinegaroon, not ten miles off."

Slocum had seen Vinegaroon, named after one of the most ugly bugs he'd ever had the misfortune to come across. The town was aptly named. He had happily ridden on, leaving it behind. Now it looked better to him than ever.

"You know what ole Phil Sheridan said about this country, don't you?"

"Haven't made a habit of followin' what Yankee generals say," Slocum allowed. He had quite a history of his own, being gut-shot by Bloody Bill Anderson after Quantrill's Raiders had killed every man and boy in Lawrence, Kansas, in retaliation for a Federal prison collapsing and killing many of the guerrillas' families. Gunning down eight-year-old boys had not appealed to him, and he had let it be known.

The bullet wounds had taken months to heal, and Slocum had dragged himself back to Slocum's Stand in Calhoun, Georgia, only to find that his parents had died. With his brother, Robert, long dead, he was sole owner of the farm—until a carpetbagger judge had taken a shine to the place.

The judge had spent most of an afternoon in the court-house making it look as if no taxes had been paid on the farm. Then he had paid the taxes out of his own pocket, thinking he could throw Slocum off and raise horses on the green, lush pastures. To this end he and a hired gunman had ridden out to evict Slocum.

At twilight, Slocum had ridden away from the farm that had been in his family for generations, leaving behind two fresh graves and a passel of wanted posters for killing a federal judge.

Not much had changed in Slocum's mind. Judges were to be tolerated—or killed. Judge Roy Bean cemented that notion firmly in his head with the way he used people for his own purposes.

"Yep, ole Phil Sheridan mighta had it right when he said if he owned Hell and Texas, he'd rent out Texas and live in Hell. This place don't budge an inch for any mother's son."

"Judge, *hola*!" cried a young Mexican boy. He came running out and threw his arms around Roy Bean.

"Here, Pepe, just for you." From the recesses of his baggy clothing, or maybe from the top of his fancy bright-red leather boots, Roy Bean pulled a shiny silver coin and handed it to the boy. "Where's your sister?"

"Elena? She is working."

"In this heat? Tell her it's siesta time. And give her this." Again Roy Bean performed his sleight-of-hand and brought forth a greenback, all folded up in a tight green square that exploded to full size as he moved theatrically.

"*Gracias*, Judge, thank you!" the boy said, a broad smile on his face. "You are the best man in the whole world."

"Yep, I surely am. Be sure to tell my partner, won't you, Pepe?" Bean nudged Slocum in the ribs and laughed.

"Oh, *señor*, he *is* a good man. He saved us when we were starving. The Comanche, they kill my parents, but the Judge helped my sister and me."

"Go tell Elena to wait 'til sundown to do that laundry. No sense for a good-looking young lady like her killin' herself in this sun."

Roy Bean walked on through Langtry, waving to people and howdying with them. Slocum watched and knew the real power the judge had in Val Verde County. He treated the locals well, but woe to the traveler in this desolate land.

Like John Slocum.

"I've raised horses, lost a brother, had a good wife and kids, done 'bout everything in the world there is worth doing, but this is my favorite. I *like* bein' justice of the peace, Slocum. I found my calling here in Langtry. Now what's the use of havin' power like this if'n I don't use it to satisfy one little harmless whim?"

"I won't kidnap her if she doesn't want to come."

"What?" bellowed Bean. "Mrs. Langtry will want to come to the town named in her honor. Don't talk foolishness. I'll telegraph ahead and let her know yer the one escortin' her back. And you'll see that not a single hair on that blessed woman's head is harmed!"

"Why me, Judge? You got men loyal to you, who'd die for you." Slocum glanced over his shoulder at the pair of deputies trailing them. They looked like hunters who'd found the spoor of a marauding coyote and were just getting it into their rifle sights.

"The boys? I trust them with my life, but they don't have the polish needed for a request like this. Somebody with a touch of sophistication is needed to invite Mrs. Langtry."

"And you chose me, a drifter with a lame horse?"

"Slocum, Slocum, you underestimate yourself. On purpose, I suspect. You got a slick Southern charm 'bout you. I hear some book learning in yer voice. You're not stupid and you ain't a bad lookin' galoot. You're just the kind of man Mrs. Langtry would listen to if you sugar coat the words."

"Why don't you go?"

"I got responsibilities," Roy Bean said almost sadly. "You might think it's an easy job ridin' herd on these ruffians. It ain't. I got a veritable epidemic of crime on my hands right now. If I could hop the train and go to San

Antone to talk to her, I would. But New Orleans is too far away. I'd be gone too long, and Langtry might fall apart. Strong hands are needed on the reins here, mark my words."

"You'll give me back my watch when I show up with her?"

"The Jersey Lily," sighed Roy Bean, rhapsodizing again. "Here in the town named after her. I kin see it now. I'll be able to die happy, hearin' her songbird voice and seein' her fine show up there on my very own stage."

Judge Roy Bean, Law West of the Pecos, motioned to a deputy who came over and thrust a handful of greenbacks into Slocum's hand. The other deputy returned Slocum's Colt Navy. It took him only a few seconds to realize it had been given back to him unloaded.

"Go to the livery and tell that worthless Gus Morton to give you a good horse. It's a powerful long way to New Orleans."

With that, Judge Roy Bean sauntered off, basking equally in the hot Texas sun and the adulation of Langtry's residents.

2

It could not get any worse, Slocum thought. He sat astride the most swayback nag he had ever seen. A glue factory would have rejected the slow-moving, rolling-gaited mare. As he traveled the dusty road to Abilene on his way to Fort Worth and eventually New Orleans, he fumed at his bad luck. Considering his alternatives, Slocum knew that finding Mrs. Lily Langtry and persuading her to return with him to the Jersey Lily Saloon for a command performance was about as likely as retrieving his brother's watch from Judge Roy Bean's clutching grasp.

The notion of circiing, sneaking back into town and stealing the watch occurred to him about twice every mile, and each time he knew it would never work. Bean was no one's fool. The watch wouldn't be kept where it would be easily found—or stolen. It might be buried in the desert or hidden away in any of a thousand other places, all beyond Slocum's reach should he try to regain what was rightfully his.

More than this, the look that had come to Bean's eye when he spoke of Lily Langtry told Slocum that this was an obsession that would not be easily erased. Steal the watch and he was likely to find Roy Bean's men on his trail for the rest of his days. Bean had the look of a man you never crossed.

Slocum patted the wad of greenbacks the judge had given him and knew it was barely enough to get to New Orleans and back. Nothing about the obsession was haphazard. Roy Bean thought it all through. Give him a few dollars more and Slocum might figure the watch was lost and the money was pay enough. Too little and Slocum would never be back with the Jersey Lily herself.

"Damn your eyes," Slocum cursed as he rode. The sun beat down on him, but his hat brim fended off the worst of the sunlight. He was sweating, but his clothes hardly had time to turn wet. The air was so dry that it sucked up any perspiration and cooled him a mite. But the cost lay in how much he drank. Two canteens of water were scarcely enough in this arid land.

"Too much," Slocum finally admitted, dismounting and leading his horse. "I can't go on and don't see how you're doing it, old girl." He patted the mare's neck. Large brown eyes turned to him as if accusing him of treachery. Even Bean's horse was single-minded about fetching Lily Langtry.

The small pool of water he found off the road proved sweet. Too much water struggling to the surface in the Big Bend region carried heavy alkali in it. He drank his fill, let the horse drink greedily, and then filled his canteens and pulled the mare away before she bloated. Slocum dropped to a patch of shade, which was rare in this country. From Langtry he had ridden due east and then curved northeast toward Fort Worth. In a couple days he would be out of the worst of the desert and into the rolling hills covered with grass that were almost as bad as the desert. Here he had mountains to guide him. On the prairie there was only the distant horizon—the same in all directions.

"Munch some of that grama," he told the horse. "Not much, I know, but when we get somewhere with a livery I'll see you get some grain." With that, he tipped his hat down over his eyes and tried to take a siesta. Barely had Slocum drifted off to a fitful sleep when the rattle of chains and the creaking of tortured wood reached him. The frightened neighs of several horses woke him up, his hand resting on the ebony butt of the six-shooter in its cross-draw holster.

Slocum climbed to the top of a rock near the watering hole and flopped belly-down to see what was going on. Not fifty yards away a stagecoach had halted. From the way the driver had his hands thrust high into the air, Slocum knew what was happening. He looked around for the highwaymen but didn't find them.

He slid back down the rock like a lizard scuttling for its hole, grabbed his Winchester from the saddle sheath and headed out to see if he could help the driver. Riding, even in one of the wallowing Concords, was better than sitting astride a saddle under the sun, riding a swaybacked horse to its grave.

Gunshots spurred Slocum to greater speed. He rounded the boulder and looked down the road where two masked men stood in the rocks. One held a smoking rifle. Not finding the driver told Slocum that the robber had blown the man out of the box. Sinking down, Slocum took cover behind a tall clump of prickly pear cactus. It wouldn't provide any shelter if the highwaymen started shooting, but it would hide him until he could figure out what was going on.

"Get out! Do it or we'll ventilate you, too!" came the shouted command from high in the rocks. Slocum located the man. Three robbers—so far.

From the coach emerged a mousy-looking man wearing a six-gun slung low on his hip in the fashion of a gunfighter. The second man looked to be a farmer. The sodbuster turned and helped a third passenger climb out.

Slocum caught his breath when he saw a lovely woman emerging amid a flutter of petticoats and skirts. When she turned, her face was drawn with tension, but she tried hard not to show how frightened she really was. Slocum might have seen a prettier woman in his day, but he couldn't remember when or where.

"Get them valuables out now," ordered one robber coming down from the rocks.

"I ain't got nuthin' but money to keep the farm runnin'," the farmer said. "I cain't give that to you. Me and the missus would—"

The robber savagely buffaloed the farmer for his impudence. He kept beating the man until his head turned to a bloody mess.

"Stop!" cried the woman, trying to stop the beating. The robber pushed her aside to keep up his thrashing. Slocum saw what was happening but cried out too late to stop it.

The mousy man's hand flew to the big Smith & Wesson on his hip. He cleared leather and fired point-blank into the robber's gut. The highwayman stiffened in surprise, looked down at his belly and then cried out, "He done kilt me, Ben!"

He dropped to his knees and then fell onto his side. The mousy man swung about, his six-shooter in a steady grip. He fired twice more at one of the other two highwaymen before their more accurate shooting cut him down. The woman turned from the farmer to the gunman and then back, a hand over her mouth.

"You murdered them both!" she cried. "You killed them!"

"The driver, too. And you're gonna be dead real quick if you don't hand over your valuables."

This set Slocum's pulse racing. Robbers usually spared women this indignity, but he guessed the two coming down from the rocks were mad at having their partner gunned down. Slocum couldn't tell if the robber had died of the belly wound, but it was likely since he wasn't even moaning now.

"Don't try it, Missy," the bandit Slocum took to be the leader ordered when the woman knelt, her hand going for the six-shooter dropped by the dead robber. She looked up, and Slocum read her expression clearly. She didn't see any but long odds in obeying. Better to die than to be raped and killed.

The two highwaymen saw her moving for the gun and lifted their rifles. Slocum had already drawn a bead on the leader. The round he got off went through the man's head, killing him instantly. The spray of blood distracted the other robber long enough for Slocum to lever in another round and get off a second shot.

This was more frantic, unaimed, intended to spook rather than to kill. It achieved its goal. The robber panicked when he realized he was being fired upon from behind and started firing wildly.

The dull report of the pistol in the woman's hand was hardly worth mentioning, except that it caught the man in the back. He grunted, said something Slocum didn't hear and turned, his rifle coming up to cover the woman.

Slocum never gave him the chance to fire. This shot caught him in the side of the head, and he joined his partners in hell.

"Whoa, wait, don't shoot!" Slocum cried when he saw the woman swinging the heavy six-gun around to cover him. "I just saved you!"

"Y-you're one of them!" she accused.

"No reason for me to kill my own partners, now is there?" asked Slocum. He kept his hands up high as he approached. "I was riding from Langtry toward Fort Worth when I stopped at a watering hole. Back there," he said, indicating the direction he had come.

"You heard the robbers and came to rescue me?" she asked skeptically.

"Didn't know I was rescuing you. Saw the driver cut down and figured I might keep owlhoots like them from killing everyone in the stagecoach. I'm glad I did. Now, if you don't trust me, that's fine. Just let me go my way."

He had seen many women who were pretty from a distance, but when he got closer they turned plain. Not this young woman. She had fire, now coming back to replace the fear, and beauty and a certain dignity to her that Slocum found lacking in most folks, man or woman.

"You'd just walk away?"

"I could have killed you, if I'd been one of their gang. I don't want any trouble." Slocum started backing away and then turned and felt the hairs on the back of his neck rise. He waited for the heavy slug from the .44 clutched in the woman's hand to blast his spine to dust. When it didn't come he walked a little faster.

"Wait!" she called. Slocum stopped, turned slowly, keeping his hands up. "You, you can't just leave me out here!"

"Thought you were doing a good job of handling the situation," Slocum said. "It took a mighty brave soul to stand up to robbers the way you did."

"I had no choice. And I know nothing about driving a team of horses. I might get one free and ride it, but I'm used to a buggy, not a bareback horse. And I'm not sure where I am."

"Mind if I put my hands down? The circulation's going away in my arms."

"Go on," she said, not sure she was making the right decision. The aim of the six-shooter never wavered from the center of Slocum's chest.

"You look like you can use that hogleg."

"I can," she said. "I just don't ride too well."

"A curious thing, that. Most women who can use a pistol are expert riders."

"What should we do?" she said, looking at the bodies at her feet.

"My name's John Slocum." He leaned his rifle against the nearest stagecoach wheel and used his handkerchief to wipe away the sweat and dust from his face.

"What? Oh, pardon me. I am so . . . flustered. I am Catherine Brookline. I was on my way from Fort Davis to Fort Worth and this . . . this . . . this!" She dropped the six-gun and put her face in her hands, weeping uncontrollably.

Somehow, she ended up with her face buried in Slocum's shoulder. The hot, wet tears soaked his shirt as he held her close. She was quite an armful. After she had cried herself out, Catherine pushed back from him and looked up into his green eyes. She had eyes bluer than the sky and hair the color of midnight. She was tanned but not turned to leather as if she had spent most of her time outdoors. Slocum didn't know but thought she was from a well-off family. Her combination of talents hinted at that.

"What are we going to do?" she asked, struggling to control her emotions. "I didn't know either of them. How can we tell their families?"

"As much as they'd like to be buried in some family cemetery plot, that's not in the cards," Slocum said, looking up. Vultures circled, spotting a decent meal waiting to rot. "You go on over to the watering hole while I bury them. The driver, too."

"What of the robbers?"

"They can share the same grave," Slocum said, seeing a considerable amount of digging in the hard, dry desert ahead of him. "I'll try to find out who they were so we can pass along their belongings—at least of the farmer and the other fellow." Slocum stared at the mousy man who had been so good with the six-shooter. He wondered if there might not be a reward out for that one.

Or for the robbers.

"I'll see if the highwaymen can be identified. If there's a reward on their heads, we can share it."

"What? No, not at all, Mr. Slocum. That would not be proper. You did, you did the . . ."

"The killing?" he finished for her.

"Well, I did shoot the one," Catherine admitted, seemingly aghast at the idea that she had taken another's life.

"Go rest. Take a siesta. It's going to be quite a spell 'fore I finish with them," he said. Catherine hesitantly left him to the distasteful chore of digging four graves, three for the driver and passengers and a larger one for the three highwaymen.

Slocum kept their belongings separate to pass along to the stagecoach agent. The agent might steal the belongings, such as they were, but that was his business. Slocum would have done the right thing. Truth was, the two passengers didn't have much between them. The farmer had a wallet stuffed with greenbacks. A quick count showed only thirty dollars. With a gold wedding band, that was his entire legacy.

The gunman had a diamond headlight stickpin and only twelve dollars in coins. His six-shooter was worth more than twelve dollars, and maybe more than the stickpin, should it turn out to be a fake. Still, even this was more than the driver had on him. The man would have had to beg someone to buy him a nickel beer at a saloon.

Aching from the work, hot and tired, Slocum made his way to the watering hole. His steps slowed, and then he stopped when he realized the woman wasn't taking a nap. She was taking a bath.

Naked.

He licked his lips and stared, knowing this wasn't too polite. But she was so danged pretty!

"John," she said, turning and seeing him. Catherine rose from the pool, naked to the waist. He could see even more of her down in the clear water. It made him uncomfortable because of the way he began to respond.

"Sorry, I didn't mean to spy on you. I thought you'd be sleeping and—"

"And you look like you could use a bath, too. How long has it been?" she asked, her eyes roving over his body in what Slocum took to be a positively provocative manner. Catherine made no effort to hide her nakedness. He saw the water running from her long, dark hair, down across the white swells of her breasts before dripping back into the pool.

"Been too long," Slocum said.

"I doubt it could be *too* long," she teased. "At least, not for me."

"Depends on what you're talking about," Slocum said, going to the edge of the pool. He sat down and kicked off his boots. He discarded his gun belt, and then the lovely woman's wet hands helped him get the rest of his clothes off until he was as bare as she was.

"Come on in," she urged. "The water's fine." Where she grabbed him to pull him into the pool was where Slocum felt the hottest—and hardest.

"That's a convenient handle for you," he observed. They moved together in the water, their damp skins rubbing sensually. Catherine whirled about, sending water everywhere, her rump pressing into the curve of his groin. She reached down between her legs and stroked over his manhood, then tugged gently, guiding it toward the spot where it would do the most good.

"Warm," Slocum said, reaching around Catherine's body. His hands came to rest naturally on her breasts. He fondled and squeezed and pulled them backward, causing the woman to press even more firmly into his groin. When Catherine bent forward, he gasped. His iron-hard length sank balls-deep into the woman's yearning chasm.

"Hot," Catherine contradicted. "You fill me up."

Slocum wasn't inclined to discuss details. His body took over, and he began moving, slowly at first and then faster and faster until they were splashing water around like a drowning dog. He held her close, their loins locked together. He loved the feel of her snowy-white buttocks pressing into him almost as much as he did the way he vanished repeatedly into the hot, tight cavern of her most intimate recess.

"Oh, yes, John. Yes, oh, yes!" the raven-haired woman cried. She screamed out her passion. Slocum groaned when the tightness around him became even tighter. It felt as if a mine shaft had collapsed on him, crushing him in the most delightful fashion possible.

This was all it took for Slocum. He spilled his seed and then sank down, floating on his back in the water. The pool was shallow, but he liked the drifting feeling provided by both the water and the sensations echoing in his body of having made love to such a beautiful woman.

"Thank you, John," Catherine said, coming to him. She rubbed her wet breasts against his chest before working down his body.

"What are you doing?"

"If you have to ask," she teased.

"We shouldn't have done this."

"You're right," she said, startling him. "We should have done *this*!" She rubbed herself all over his body, and then her lips found his flaccid length and began working on it. Before Slocum knew it, they were again making love in the water.

He hadn't expected any reward for rescuing the stage-coach from the robbers. Now he couldn't imagine how much money he'd need to get to equal this fine treasure.

3

"I can't believe the Butterfield agent gave us so much money," marveled Catherine Brookline, riffling through the thick wad of greenbacks given them in Abilene for the return of the stage.

Slocum was even happier with the reward for the Jackson gang. The federal marshal had found wanted posters on the three highwaymen amounting to more than three hundred dollars. Giving Catherine the reward for the stage, almost as much, seemed a fair division. But now their paths would part, and Slocum found himself wishing they could travel on a bit farther, sharing one another's company.

If it hadn't been for his brother's watch being held hostage by Judge Roy Bean, Slocum would have taken his reward money and drifted north, to Dodge or some other thriving cow town where gamblers plied their trade and drunk cowboys didn't know the odds.

"I need to find my brother," Catherine said, her bright blue eyes fixed on him. "It's a great deal to ask of you, John, but we *have* been through so much."

He felt a stirring he didn't much like. It never paid to think with his gonads rather than his brain, but Catherine Brookline was a lovely woman, and what they had shared on the trail was more than a blanket.

"Where's your brother?" he heard himself asking. Then his heart caught in his throat when she answered.

"Fort Worth."

"Funny about that," he said, grinning broadly. "That happens to be the direction I'm heading." He had been close-mouthed about his mission to New Orleans to convince Mrs. Lily Langtry that she ought to return with him to Langtry to perform for Roy Bean. It was downright embarrassing, and things had been going real well between him and Catherine. He didn't want her to get the idea he was nothing but an errand boy for a tinhorn justice of the peace.

He was rewarded even more by her bright smile and the real excitement on her face.

"I'm *so* glad, John. I had not wanted to make the trip alone and, well, taking the stagecoach doesn't strike me as safe as it once did."

He had to laugh. "The highwaymen are dead," he pointed out.

"There are so many more in Texas. We'd have to go past Fort Griffith, and I have heard the tales of *that* town."

It was about the biggest hellhole in Texas, and the stage route went smack through it. But if they rode, they could avoid the town and go right on into Fort Worth. From there, he could see Catherine safely in her brother's hands. He sighed, thinking that the remainder of the trip to New Orleans would not be anywhere as interesting.

"I'll get a buggy and—"

"And nothing. Two horses," the dark-haired woman insisted. "I can ride passably well, and it will be faster. I have seen the roads. They are terrible in places, nothing but sticky mud and deep ruts."

"If you can stay in the saddle, that'll get us to Fort Worth a powerful lot faster," he allowed. She touched his arm, and he knew the next week or so would be fine.

And it was. Catherine Brookline proved an able horsewoman, if a bit shaky at the start. He found her a steady mare that the woman took to right away. They arrived in Fort Worth almost too soon for Slocum's taste.

"Cattle. I do declare. They are everywhere," Catherine said, looking around as they rode past the stockyards to the north of town, angling in so they would pass Hell's Half Acre. Slocum didn't want to expose her to that kind of iniquity, although what they had done every night out on the prairie would have curled the hair of even the most hardened cyprian. Somehow, it had all seemed right as they were doing it. Looking back, Slocum wondered why he had not found a woman like Catherine Brookline earlier.

And now he had to turn her over to her family. It seemed a great loss.

"Where's your brother likely to stay?" he asked.

"What do you mean?" she asked sharply. Too sharply, Slocum thought.

"What's his business? Does he have a house or does he stay at a hotel?"

"Oh, I see," Catherine said. "Well, Davy enjoys a rather flamboyant lifestyle I do not share. He is likely to stay at the more expensive places."

"We'll try the eastern side of town," Slocum decided.

"I remember him mentioning the Transcontinental Hotel," she said, eyeing him. "At Belknap and Houston."

Slocum pictured the place in his mind. It was at the extreme north end of Hell's Half Acre, not far from the Tarrant County courthouse. This wasn't the kind of place a respectable man would stay, but Slocum said nothing. He had a feeling that Catherine wasn't telling him everything about her brother. This worried him until he realized he had told her nothing at all about why he was on his way to New Orleans.

Neither was being overly honest with the other.

"We're not far," Slocum said, turning his pony's face in the right direction. He tugged on the trailing reins of the swayback mare Bean had given him. Tending two horses was a chore, but they had made good time from Abilene because he had purchased another mount along with Catherine's. He figured he could return Roy Bean's horse and keep the paint he now rode once he returned to Langtry.

"It'll be good to see Davy again," Catherine said. "Our parents died a while back, and I've been out seeing the world."

"West Texas?"

"It's unlike anything I had ever seen before," she said almost primly. "If I am to broaden my education, I have to see places I might avoid otherwise."

"You see El Paso?" he asked, amused.

"Why, yes. What a . . . place," Catherine finished lamely. "I was rather happy to leave it behind. Fort Davis is quite nice, once you get through Wild Rose Pass. That Colonel Grierson—the post commander—is an especially nice gentleman."

Slocum wondered why Catherine was traveling alone. This wasn't done, at least by proper young ladies. Then he smiled to himself. What they had done together was hardly proper, but it surely had been fun. She had not learned it in any finishing school he had ever heard of.

"Davy and I are going back to St. Louis. Our uncle has a mercantile and has offered us positions. I can keep the books and Davy is perfect as manager. We—oh, there it is. The hotel." Catherine pointed south down Throckmorton to the three-story-tall Transcontinental Hotel. It took Slocum a few more minutes before he saw the sign hanging in front. The only way Catherine could have known this was the right place was if she had been here before.

Slocum pushed the niggling thought from his mind as he dismounted and then helped her jump to the ground. She rubbed her rump and shook her head, causing a small spray of dark hair to form over her head. The setting sun caught it and turned it into a halo.

"I am certainly glad to be out of the saddle," she said, smoothing her skirts before climbing the short flight of steps to the hotel lobby. The cut glass doors reflected rainbows as she opened the door and went in amid a swirl of skirts. Slocum followed.

"Good afternoon, sir," she said to the desk clerk. The seedy man stood and leered at her until he spotted Slocum standing behind her. The leer vanished and a pained expression replaced it.

"How can I help you?" the clerk asked sourly. "You want a room?"

"Rooms," Slocum broke in. "If we can find her brother."

"Yes, Davy Brookline," Catherine said. "He always stays here."

"Brookline?" The man scratched his stubbled chin and shook his head. "Don't think we got anyone here by that name."

"I'll make sure," Slocum said, spinning the room register around. He flipped back through a half dozen pages until he decided the clerk was right.

"He's not here?" Catherine asked, eyes wide. "But where else would I find him? Unless . . ." Her voice trailed off.

"Where?" Slocum demanded. He had a bad feeling about this. The hotel wasn't too bad, but any farther south would take them into treacherous territory, the kind of place where Slocum walked with his hand resting on the butt of his six-shooter.

"He has a yen to gamble. It was a weakness he shared with our father. And Davy also imbibed," she said almost sadly. "To excess. Too often.

"If he's taken to drinking again, there's no telling where he might have gone."

Slocum looked at the clerk, who stared at Catherine intently.

"What is it?" Slocum demanded of the clerk.

"There was a fellow that come in here a week or so back wanting a room. Didn't have enough money to spend the night, so I throwed him out. But he looked a bit like you.

The hair was the same color, the eyes were blue, but his hair was receding something fierce. Had a nasty scar across his chin, otherwise was a decent enough looking guy."

Slocum saw how this hit Catherine. Her lips pursed into an O and then her hand covered her mouth.

"That's Davy," she said.

"He said something about losing his money at John Leer's Place. That's the Comique Saloon down on Eighth Street. Just take Houston south until you get to it. A real busy watering hole."

"We'll get settled first. You got *two* rooms for the lady and me?" Slocum asked.

"Sure thing. Sign right here. Or make your mark."

Slocum and Catherine signed the register and then Slocum lugged their gear upstairs. Their rooms were across the hall from one another. Catherine hesitated, staring at him with her blue, blue eyes, and then said, "It's a waste of money getting two rooms, John."

"I don't want folks talking," Slocum said. "You have a reputation to maintain."

For some reason, this struck Catherine as funny. She stopped laughing after a few seconds and reached out to lay her soft, warm hand on his arm.

"You are such a gentleman, John. How are we going to find Davy?"

"*I'll* go see what I can. This saloon is no place for you. Only soiled doves are likely to go there."

"Soiled doves," Catherine said, rolling the words over and over on her tongue, as if she savored the taste. "What an odd way to describe a whore. Don't look shocked, John. I have learned so much on my trip through the West."

"It's no place for you," he insisted.

"I ought to go, to help you find him."

"The description the clerk gave ought to be good enough for me to see if anyone remembers Davy," he said. They stood in the hall for a moment, then Catherine rose on tiptoes and lightly kissed him on the lips.

"I'll be waiting for you. And I hope you don't put your bed to *too* much use tonight." The raven-haired lovely smiled lasciviously and then spun and went into her room. Slocum heaved a sigh. Going to a dive in the middle of one of the worst hellholes in Texas wasn't what he wanted to do right now.

But if he found her brother, Catherine might be even more grateful. He stowed his gear, went downstairs and led their horses to a stable down the street, and then set out for the Comique Saloon.

It was exactly where the clerk had said, a ramshackle place with the saloon downstairs, gambling tables in the back room and cribs upstairs. Painted women went up a broad staircase with their customers, but during the fifteen minutes or so that Slocum watched he never saw one of the women come down with the man she had gone up with.

He knew if he went to the rear of the saloon he would find the back stairs and a pile of drunk, robbed cowboys. They'd sober up in the morning with an aching head and empty pockets and think they'd had the time of their lives the night before.

Slocum nursed a warm beer that tasted like iodine as he studied the men in the saloon. None matched the description of Catherine's brother. Slocum drifted to the rear room with its green felt-covered gaming tables. Two were occupied with cowboys trying to outbluff each other. At both were shifty-eyed gamblers intent on raking in as much from the cowboys as they could. It took Slocum less than a minute to see how the gamblers were cheating. He moved on, bored.

"Well, hello," said a scrawny woman with fever-bright eyes. She ran her hand up and down his arm. "My, aren't you a strong one? How about we go upstairs for some fun?"

Slocum reckoned the woman spent all her money on laudanum. Too much of the opiate stole away weight ounce by ounce, pound by pound, and produced the too-bright eyes he looked into now. He reached into his pocket and drew out a five-dollar bill.

Her eyes went wide.

"I only get two bits," she blurted. Then she licked her lips and said, "I mean, I don't bite much. That's about right for the time of your life, honey chile."

Slocum moved the greenback just out of her grasping hand.

"Not so fast. I'm paying for something special."

"It's yours. You want a couple other girls? I can—"

"Information is all I'm after," Slocum said, feeling sorry for the woman. This much money might give her the wherewithal to kill herself with drugs. He didn't know if that might not be for the best.

"Hey, I'm not gonna peach on Cassady. He'd rip my heart out and shove it down my throat if I did." She stepped back and looked hard at Slocum. "You don't look like the law."

Slocum snorted at this. He had more than one wanted poster floating around the West. Killing the carpetbagger judge back in Georgia had only been the start of a checkered career that often crossed the line of legality.

"I'm looking for a friend by the name of Davy Brookline."

"Davy? You're a friend of his?" The soiled dove laughed harshly. "He stiffed me. He owes damned near every son of a bitch in this place and up and down Houston Street."

"Where do I find him?" Slocum asked, not sure if he wanted to hear the answer. The woman was so vehement about the way Davy had cheated her and others that Catherine's brother might have ended up as buzzard food out on the prairie. There wasn't a man in the Comique Saloon who wouldn't backshoot a man welshing on a gambling debt.

She shifted her gaze from Slocum's face to the greenback. He wondered if she was thinking up a good lie or if she'd tell the truth—and whether he could tell the difference. The woman glanced around and then took the five dollar bill from his fingers.

"I don't know for sure, but I heard him say he was getting out of town pronto."

"Where?" Slocum asked. "Where did he say he was headed?"

"New Orleans," the woman said.

Slocum returned to the Transcontinental Hotel, whistling a jaunty tune as he went.

4

Slocum lounged back in the railroad passenger car, eyes shut, letting the rolling motion soothe him. This was better than riding endless miles across the east Texas piney woods only to find he had gone a scant dozen miles. The train from Fort Worth rambled across the Mississippi and directly down into New Orleans. He had not liked the notion of stabling the horses in Fort Worth. Better to have sold them, but he worried that Judge Roy Bean might have some peculiar attachment to the swayback nag he had given him.

The last thing in the world Slocum wanted was to cross the contrary judge. For a justice of the peace in a jerkwater town like Langtry, Bean wielded a whale of a lot of influence.

Slocum pushed back his hat and looked at the seat across from him. Catherine Brookline sat, hands in her lap, staring out the window at the countryside passing by so rapidly. They would be in New Orleans within the hour, and Slocum would likely never see her again. Somehow, this bothered him more than it ought to.

She was wild and exciting when they were alone and demure in public. About the perfect woman, Slocum thought. It seemed odd she was so driven to find her brother. From what Slocum could tell, Davy Brookline was

31

a wastrel and more than likely going to end up on the wrong end of a gun. Still, he knew that blood was thicker than water. He had bailed out more than one relative— distant ones, to boot—and never counted the cost. Davy was Catherine's only sibling, so he would be like a magnet pulling her to help.

"It won't be long. I recognize the river," Catherine said. The train cautiously made its way across a long bridge spanning the Mississippi River.

"Not many rivers this big," Slocum allowed. "See it once and you never forget it." He studied Catherine's fine features, the cascade of her dark hair over her shoulders, the way she moved, everything about her. It wasn't going to be possible to forget her.

Some things, like the broad, muddy Mississippi, were unforgettable.

"I'm not exactly sure where to look for him in New Orleans. Could you help me, John? You've done so much for me, I hate to ask."

"I have to see to some business first. If you haven't located Davy by the time I'm finished, I'd be glad to help."

"Meeting you has been about the best thing to happen to me in years," Catherine said earnestly, laying a hand warmly on his leg. Slocum said nothing, enjoying her proximity. Before he knew it, the train pulled into the depot north of town, and it was time for them to go their separate ways.

"I'll stay at the Regent Hotel, just outside Congo Square," Catherine told him. He was amazed at her knowledge of the cities they came to. It had been as if she had a map of Fort Worth etched in her mind. New Orleans might have been her home from her easy way of figuring out where to stay and how to go about hunting for her brother.

"Take care," he advised. "This can be a rough town."

"I'll miss you, John," she said. Impulsively kissing him, Catherine backed off, flushed. She bit her lower lip, batted

her eyes at him, then hurried away without another word.
Slocum watched her vanish into the crush of passengers
from the train. It ought to have felt like the end of the trail.
It didn't.

He pushed this feeling aside, intending to reach Lily
Langtry as quickly as he could so he could ransom his
brother's watch from Roy Bean and be on his way again.
Being beholden to the judge was not something he cottoned
to much.

The only bright spot was that Lily ought to have received
Bean's telegram by now and would be ready to make the
trip across Texas to the Mexican border for her command
performance. Slocum neither knew nor cared what entice-
ment Bean offered her. The celebrity-struck justice of the
peace had a persuasive manner Slocum could not deny.

The American Quarter, with its antebellum mansions and
obvious wealth, lay on the west side of Canal Street. Along
the broad street were dozens of theaters, catering to New
Orleans denizens from both sides of Canal. Here the rich
mingled with the not-so-rich. And it was here, just above
Royal Street, where Slocum found a marquee prominently
detailing the tour of the famous Jersey Lily herself, Lily
Langtry.

Going around to the rear of the theater to the stage door,
Slocum cautiously poked his head inside. A few stagehands
struggled to get scenery into place. Otherwise, no one was
about. Slocum went in and stood in shadow for a few
minutes, watching the three men working to get the set
erected.

One finally noticed him.

"Whatchya doin' heah?" the tallest and rangiest of the
three men asked. "Nobody's 'lowed backstage."

"I need to speak with Mrs. Langtry."

"You 'n' a millyun othahs," the stagehand said, laughing.
"She ain't heah and won't be 'til the show. Talk to her
manager."

Slocum looked in the direction the man pointed and saw

a small door set in the side wall. He opened it and found himself in a low, narrow passageway around the proscenium leading toward the front of the theater. Hurrying down it, feeling like a cow in a dipping chute, Slocum came out in the front lobby.

"What do you want?" demanded a man coming out of the manager's office.

"I've been sent for Mrs. Langtry."

"Sent? What are you talking about? There's nothing wrong with her, is there? I got the whole damn theater sold out tonight. I'm not—"

"There's nothing wrong with her, that I know," Slocum said. "Judge Roy Bean sent her a telegram about a . . . command performance after she leaves New Orleans. I'm here to escort her to the Jersey Lily."

Slocum pictured the ramshackle saloon and tried to keep from laughing at the notion. This was a fancy theater with sets and a big stage and well nigh three hundred seats padded for the comfort of its patrons' backsides. Comparing that with a gin mill that might have two straight-backed wood chairs that wouldn't collapse and a stage that looked more like a parody of this place was a futile pursuit.

Judge Roy Bean was not to be denied. If Lily Langtry went along with it, who was Slocum to mock either of them?

"Mr. Glencannon!" bellowed the manager. "You got a visitor out here in the lobby."

From inside the manager's office came a dapper man with a small, greased mustache and hair so oiled back he reeked. He wore an expensive suit and carried a thick sheaf of papers.

"What is it?"

"You know anything about this fellow's claim that he's here to escort Lily?"

"Escort her?" scoffed the well-dressed man. "Of course not." He looked Slocum over from head to toe and then sneered. "She does not consort with such ruffians. It is bad enough they are even allowed in the audience."

"They pay their admission, they get in," the theater manager said belligerently.

"Yes, yes, of course, old chap. I know that. You," Glencannon said, pinning Slocum with a steely gaze. "What is your business?"

"Who are you?"

The two men exchanged glances. The theater manager shrugged and vanished into the bowels of his lavish establishment. Glencannon straightened, struck a pose and said, "I am Mrs. Langtry's business manager, and I do not know you."

"She got a telegram from Judge Bean," Slocum said, not liking the way the conversation was going. "He arranged for her to go to Langtry, Texas, for a performance."

"You jest, sir."

"I'm here to escort her to Langtry. Judge Roy Bean's named the whole town after her, in her honor."

"How special," Glencannon said, sneering even more now. "I know nothing of such an arrangement. From here we travel on a riverboat—first cabin, of course—to Baton Rouge. I assure you we are *not* going to Texas again. The performance in Houston was utterly wretched. How a woman of her sensibilities endured that, I cannot say."

"Let me talk to her and—" Slocum cut off the words when he saw the theater manager return with the three stagehands. They carried pry bars and short wood staves, slapping them against their palms as if testing them to see how a blow might feel—against Slocum's head.

"You will not talk to her. You will remove yourself immediately from these premises," Glencannon said pompously, "and if you do not, woe will befall you!" He struck a pose, one hand on his lapel, the other thrust in the air as if he carried a sword.

"Where's she staying? I can clear this up. Maybe she got the telegram and never told you," Slocum suggested. Before the last word left his lips, he found himself on the receiving end of a swinging length of steel. The pain that shot through his arm spun him about. A wood stave hit him in the chest and another blow behind the knees knocked him to the floor.

"Throw him out. In the alley, not out front, you fools," snapped the theater manager.

Slocum felt himself dragged back along the narrow corridor and then tumbled down the short flight of steps behind the theater.

"Now, don't go comin' back. This heah time we been gentle with ya," the stagehand said. "You go gettin' folk riled and we git tough with yo' haid."

The slamming door was followed with the solid sound of a locking bar dropping into place. Slocum moaned and forced himself to sit up. Every muscle in his body screamed in agony. Rubbing his arm, Slocum got some circulation back. It took longer before he could walk.

Getting Mrs. Lily Langtry to her command performance west of the Pecos was going to be harder than he thought.

Damn Bean!

"I'll give you a dollar to buy a ticket for me," Slocum asked a passerby along Canal Street. The man furtively looked around and then down at the well-used Colt Navy in Slocum's holster.

"Why not buy it yourself?" the man asked.

"They won't sell me one," Slocum said, not wanting to go into the long, convoluted story. He had tried to get a ticket to Lily Langtry's evening performance but had been chased off when the manager saw him. Slocum wasn't sure how getting to see and hear the Jersey Lily on stage would help, but he had to do something.

"Save your money, friend," the man said. "Sold out. And if I got a ticket, I'd use it. She's about the best warbler in the whole danged world."

Disgusted with this turn of fate, Slocum paced in front of the theater hoping to buy a ticket. No one was selling for any amount he could afford. When three armed men came out, Slocum knew he was barking up the wrong tree. He needed a little time to think how to reach the woman with Roy Bean's fervent invitation. Slocum couldn't think of any reason he shouldn't pass some of that time with Catherine Brookline.

"The Regent," he muttered to himself, setting off to find the hotel. It took the better part of an hour to find it, not a block from Congo Square. Despite its fancy name, the hotel was right on the edge of being disreputable. And the neighborhood gave Slocum pause. He walked the night streets around the hotel with every sense straining, waiting for trouble to find him.

He entered the lobby and found a moderately better interior than was suggested by the exterior.

"Miss Catherine Brookline," he inquired of the room clerk. The man's rheumy eyes barely focused, and Slocum knew he had been tippling.

"Not in," the clerk said.

"I'll wait." Slocum flopped in a chair that commanded a view of both the stairs leading to the second floor and the front door. It was early yet. He wasn't sure when he might expect Catherine, but it ought to be before midnight. In the meantime, he could work out how best to speak with Mrs. Langtry about what was looking like a trip she not only had no knowledge of but wouldn't likely want to take even if she did.

Slocum had been in the chair scarcely fifteen minutes when a distraught Catherine Brookline came into the hotel lobby.

"Catherine!" he called. It took her a second to realize someone had called her name. When she saw him, she rushed to him and buried her face in his shoulder and began crying. "What's wrong?"

"It's Davy," she sobbed. "I found him, but he . . . he's *drunk*."

From what she had said before, he wondered why this was such a surprise.

"Is there anything I can do?" he heard himself asking. Slocum bit his lip, wanting to take back the question but knew he couldn't.

"Would you get him out of that terrible place? It's down in the Vieux Carré, a place on Gallatin Street. I can't remember the saloon's name."

"I know the area," he said. The street was not far from Lafayette Square and was lined with dozens of dives. "Go to your room and I'll see to fetching him for you."

"Will you know him?"

"The scar on his chin," Slocum said. "And he must look something like you," he went on. Catherine's head bobbed up and down in assent. She looked up, her bright blue eyes bloodshot from crying, and he knew he could never deny her. It hardly mattered he had to speak with Lily Langtry about performing for Roy Bean. This wouldn't take more than an hour or so.

"Thank you, John. I *do* appreciate this."

She hugged him and then ran up the stairs, crying again. Slocum heaved a deep sigh and set off across town for the little piece of hell calling itself Gallatin Street.

Slocum went past the Web, a saloon near Poydras on Franklin Street, and then stopped and peered into the smoky interior. He had checked other saloons along Gallatin without finding Davy Brookline, but that meant nothing. He had never seen the man and might have missed him, but Slocum didn't think so. Those places were almost orderly, the bouncers keeping the drunken brawls to a minimum. From the way Catherine had reacted, he suspected her brother was kicking up his heels and presenting a first-class menace to anyone getting near him.

A man in the corner of the Web caught Slocum's eye. He stood on a chair and shouted obscenities at anyone daring to come close. He had a half-full bottle of tarantula juice in his hand and, between tirades against everyone in the saloon, he worked to drain it.

Slocum stepped inside and edged along the exterior wall at his back for protection. Unlike the other joints, the Web didn't pay for a bouncer. This turned the place into a free-for-all that no one seemed to mind. Getting closer, Slocum studied the man on the chair. He was dressed in what had once been decent clothing but was now shabby and tattered through neglect. But the shape of his face, the midnight dark hair, the bright blue eyes—and the large pink scar on his chin—told him he had found Catherine's brother.

"Davy, it's time to go," Slocum said loudly. He looked up at the man, now both drunk and startled.

"How'd ya know who I am?"

"Your sister's worried about you."

"Catherine's here?" The man looked around, his arms flailing wildly.

"Not here," Slocum said. "At her hotel. Let's go and—"

"I don' know you!" Davy shouted. "You're tryin' to r-rob me!"

"No!" Slocum shouted. He had two choices. He could throw down the man as he clumsily pulled out a heavy .44 from under his jacket, but Slocum didn't want to kill him. Or he could get out of the way. Which he did, diving under a nearby table as the heavy pistol erupted. Davy Brookline fired wildly, not knowing if he had a decent target.

Lead flying, Slocum peered around the edge of the table he had overturned. His heart skipped a beat when he saw a brute of a man waddle toward Davy, oblivious to the gunfire.

"You put that thang down," the man bellowed, "or I'll ram it up yo' ass!"

Those were the last words the man ever spoke. Davy's sixth slug caught him smack in the middle of his broad, ugly face. Amid a shower of blood and brains, the man staggered back and fell flat on the floor, dead before he crashed down to the sawdust.

A sudden hush fell over the saloon. Then a voice cried, "He done kilt Big Ed. The Spiders'll massacre the lot of us! Ed was Yellow Henry's favorite!"

Slocum stood, looked around at an empty room and realized Davy Brookline had murdered a member of one of New Orleans's more infamous gangs. The Spiders specialized in robbing Negro businesses and were not above murder, just for the fun of it. As an act of retribution, every Spider in New Orleans would be out for blood.

He heard the sharp bleat of police whistles along Poydras and knew there wasn't much time. In New Orleans, the police were as likely to be members of the gang as they were to enforce the law.

Either way, Davy was in a world of trouble.

Slocum spun to call to the man and stared at the empty chair where Davy had stood. Slocum was alone in the Web and felt as if he had been plunged into a vise that was closing in all around him.

5

Slocum spun, his hand flashing for his six-shooter. He got off a round as a scrawny, rat-faced man burst through the front doors of the Web carrying a double-barreled shotgun. The double-ought buckshot from the shotgun and the .36 slug from Slocum's six-gun crossed in midair. In spite of the greater number of pellets, the gunman missed his target.

Slocum didn't.

He crouched as a shower of plaster from the wall behind rained down on him and then knew he couldn't stay in the saloon a second longer. He had just plugged what was likely to be another of the Spider gang's members. Slocum had no idea who Yellow Henry might be, and he didn't want to find out. Duck-walking to keep a low profile, he found the back door Davy Brookline must have used to escape so fast. The alley was littered with debris and piles of rotting garbage.

Slocum hardly noticed as he ran as hard as he could to get away from the saloon that had become a slaughterhouse in the wink of an eye. Thrusting his six-shooter back into his holster, Slocum stepped out onto Poydras Street and looked around. It looked as if someone had poured boiling water down an anthill. Men exploded from other saloons and dance halls, all intent on busting heads. Some carried ax handles. Others cut the air with knives. Still others showed their expertise with sling shots used on each other.

The brawls abated when a mountain of a man shoved his way through the crowd. Slocum knew he ought to hightail it, but some perverse curiosity held him in place to watch the spectacle unfold.

The man was as big around as he was tall and looked like a fleshy ball rolling along through the crowd. Arms thicker than Slocum's thighs shoved others aside until he reached the door into the Web. A shock of bright yellow hair told Slocum this had to be Yellow Henry, the leader of the Spiders.

"Big Ed's dead. This here's Add's body. Some son of a bitch shot him, too. Who done it? Gimme a name! Gimme a name and I'll see you get rich. Don't tell me and I'll damn well kill you!"

The bull-throated roar echoed up one street and down the other in the Vieux Carré. Time seemed to stand still. The quiet that descended was so intense, the only noise Slocum heard was the hammering of his own heart. He wanted to back away and get to safety—wherever that might be. But moving a muscle now would draw unwanted attention to him.

Slocum didn't think any of the gang knew he had even been in the Web, but he didn't want to take the chance.

"Who done it? Nobody kills *two* members of *my* gang and lives to brag about it. Who?" The question billowed from deep in the man's barrel-chest and sent those closest to him reeling back.

"I heard tell the gent's name was Davy," spoke up one man. A riverman, from the look of his clothing, seconded that. Slocum held his breath, waiting for anyone to furnish a last name.

"Davy Brookline," said the barkeep in a clear voice. "He welshed on some gambling debts and got so stinkin' drunk he didn't know what the hell he was doin'."

"I don't care. He's dead," Yellow Henry declared.

"There was another fellow huntin' for him. Don't know his moniker. Tall, wore his six-shooter in a cross-draw holster. Had the look of big trouble."

"I want him dead, too. I want anyone dead who even *spoke* to Davy Brookline!"

A cheer rose up that chilled Slocum. He had seen law-abiding citizens whip themselves into a frenzy before lynching a man. Not a man on the street tonight could by any stretch of the imagination be declared law abiding. If the mouth of hell opened right at this moment and swallowed the lot of them, New Orleans would be without crime until new cutthroats and pirates came to replace them.

Slocum whipped off his hat so no one would recognize it and looked at the street, trying to appear short and insignificant as the maddened crowd surged past him. He went with them until he came to another alley that afforded a moment's peace and a chance to think. Wiping sweat off his forehead, he compared the hot, humid night to the dusty dryness of west Texas.

In spite of Judge Roy Bean, Slocum wished he was in Langtry and not New Orleans right now. Being fed to the judge's pet bear seemed a kinder fate than he was likely to get at the hands of Yellow Henry's gang.

Slocum felt some obligation to find Davy for his sister's sake, but to do so would put his own hide in jeopardy. The Spiders knew Davy's name. No one knew him. Yet. The barkeep might identify him, but that was a long shot if Slocum simply left New Orleans.

He cursed when he realized how little he had accomplished since coming to the Crescent City. He had not even gotten past Lily's manager. Now Catherine's brother was in danger of being strung up—or more likely, worse—and Slocum might be able to prevent it. All he had to do was find the man before the mob did.

Slocum grunted. He knew where his duty lay, but it rankled him. It also might get him killed.

He set out hunting for Davy Brookline.

• • •

The farther he got from the Web, the fewer unusual activities Slocum spotted. Still, New Orleans at night was a treacherous place for the unwary. He moved through the crowds, trying to think like Davy Brookline. Where would the man run? As drunk as Davy had been, Slocum didn't think he could have gotten too far. And it was doubtful he knew of the manhunt mounted for him by Yellow Henry and his gang.

Slocum went into a smoky, noisy dance hall along Gallatin Street and studied the crowd. Leon's Fireproof Coffeehouse was inappropriately named, Slocum thought, seeing how the wormy wood walls were tinder dry and the sawdust on the floor smoldered from dropped cigars. And if coffee was ever served within these four walls, it was laced with potent brandy or whiskey concocted with nitric acid in the back room.

"You're cheatin', damn your eyes!" came an aggrieved cry from the corner of the room. Ordinarily, Slocum would have discounted it. Cheating—and accusations of cheating—were so commonplace as to be easily ignored. But not this time. The voice that responded struck a chord with him.

Slocum turned and looked through the blue-gray smoke that hung like a choking fog at the table. A riverman pushed back from the table, brawny hands gripping the edge as he levered himself erect on shaky legs. Slocum couldn't see the man he accused across the table, but the voice was familiar. Too familiar.

"You don't know nuthin'," said Davy Brookline. "Here. Look at this." He dropped his heavy six-shooter on the table. "My iron friend here says you're full of it. You been out on that there muddy river so long you don't know that a flush beats a straight."

"You don't have no flush! That's a red card." The riverman's finger stabbed down on the cards Davy had laid in front of him. "You just smudged it to look like a black card."

Davy lifted the six-shooter and cocked it. The riverman backed off, and then his resolve hardened. No one was going to cheat him. Slocum read the promise of mayhem on the man's face and knew Davy did not. He was still too drunk.

"Go on and shoot me, you swindlin' tinhorn gambler!" raged the riverman.

Slocum swallowed when Davy pulled the trigger. The hammer fell on a spent chamber. He had not bothered reloading since he had fired all six rounds back in the Web. Slocum and the riverman moved as one, heading for Davy Brookline.

Slocum got there first, grabbing Davy and spinning him around. "You cheated me! I want my money!"

"Wha? Who the hell are you?" Davy asked, his eyes not focusing. "I never saw you before in my life!"

"You," Slocum barked, summoning up his best command voice as he shouted at the riverman. He had been a captain in the CSA and knew how to issue orders. "Take the pot. It's yours. I'm going to beat out of him what he owes me."

"I want—" started the riverman, wanting a fight more than his money. He found himself staring down the barrel of Slocum's Colt Navy. He realized he wasn't likely to see a repeat of the hammer falling on an empty cylinder. The man scooped up his money and backed off.

Fight? Yes, heartily. Die? Some other day.

Slocum swung around to face Davy and found that he had again sneaked away. Davy might be drunk, but he was slipperier than a greased eel. The path he had blazed through the crowd to the front door was only just closing. Slocum hurried after him, overtaking him just outside the dance hall.

Slocum grabbed and caught Davy's collar, yanking him around.

"Half of the gangs in New Orleans are hunting for you with blood in their eyes," Slocum told the drunk. "If you don't go to ground, you're going to end up floating face down in the Mississippi."

"Who are you?" Davy peered at him, then closed one eye to focus better. "I remember you. Back in that other saloon."

"Your sister sent me to find you. You left Fort Worth in a hurry. I can figure out why real easy. Why she wants you back is something I can't figure out at all."

"Catherine's here? Where?" Davy looked around and then slipped free of Slocum's grip and ran down the street, dodging other drunks with an ease Slocum found hard to match.

He bounced from one to another, getting cursed at and sometimes punched. Slocum kept running, slowly overtaking Davy. The drunkard's wind broke, and he tumbled to the street, allowing Slocum to catch him again.

"You're a fool. I don't know how you deserve such a fine sister as Catherine."

"She's got you hooked, don't she?" Davy laughed. "She's like that. She—"

Slocum punched him. This sobered Davy for a moment.

"Yellow Henry and the Spiders want your blood. You killed Big Ed. You remember that?"

"Who's Big Ed?"

Slocum shook his head. Davy had blacked out on much of what he had done. Too much liquor did that, or maybe it was just a way he had come to deal with the world. Slocum had seen other men, cold-blooded killers, who couldn't remember who they had just sent to the cemetery. It might not have mattered to most of them, but they put their misdeeds out of their minds right away.

"There, there they are. Both of 'em," came a cry from behind. Slocum recognized the barkeep from the Web. He was the only one able to link him with Davy. And now it looked as if half the Spiders were pounding down the street, intent on bashing in their heads with ax handles.

"Run," Slocum said, pulling Davy to his feet. "That's the Spider gang."

"Why are you helping me?"

"I told you. Your sister wants you kept alive, though why is beyond me."

"I don't believe you. This is a trick. You said I owed you money. I heard you back in that gin mill."

"That was to keep the riverman from beating you to death," Slocum said, knowing explanations as they ran were useless. Too many of Yellow Henry's gang were hot in pursuit for him to take the time to convince Davy of his sincerity.

Davy suddenly changed directions, taking Slocum by surprise. Before Slocum could skid to a halt and follow him, the Spiders passed the mouth of the alley where Davy had taken refuge. Cut off from Catherine's brother, Slocum could only keep running.

He ran toward the levee and then cut northwest along the river. The docks ahead at the foot of Tchoupitoulas Street afforded a chance for Slocum to angle back up toward Canal Street, where the more sedate crowds might save him. Panting hard, still hearing footsteps behind him, he lowered his head and ran for all he was worth. There was no way in hell he could hope to fight it out with so many gang members.

And if he started shooting, he would likely draw the New Orleans police like flies to a fresh cow pie. Dealing with them might be worse than convincing Yellow Henry that he had nothing to do with Big Ed's death.

Slocum had no chance of even talking with the gang leader about the shotgun-wielding man's death. That had been self-defense, but Yellow Henry wasn't likely to be interested in the truth.

Cutting between warehouses, Slocum started circling back to let the gang go off on a wild goose chase. He settled down and caught his breath, hearing their thudding feet vanish into the distance. More composed, Slocum headed toward Canal street and its crush of crowds.

He had barely stepped out, near Chartres, when he spotted Davy Brookline sauntering along as if he owned the city. The man was glad handing men he could not possibly know and kissing women's hands, much to their delight and the chagrin of their escorts.

"Davy!" Slocum called and immediately regretted it. He might have lost the Spiders on his trail. Davy had not. Calling out the man's name focused the gang on their quarry again.

Four men closed in on him, knives flashing in the gaslights along the street. Slocum never considered the odds. He simply acted.

His six-shooter came out, and he shot one man in the chest, sending him backward into his partner. A cry went up in the throngs along Canal. Slocum saw the other two spiders closing on Davy, intent on cutting his throat.

He leveled his six-shooter and started to shoot, but the rush of a half dozen men and women between him and his target forced Slocum to lower the hammer on his six-gun. Pushing through, he got to Davy's side. The man fought ineffectively against the two Spiders. One held his legs and the other tried to draw his knife across Davy's throat. The first two stabs had missed, only opening wounds on Davy's arms and shoulder.

Slocum hauled off and landed a haymaker in the knife-wielder's belly. This caused the other man to release Davy's feet and go for a hidden weapon. Slocum wasn't sure what the man reached for. It might have been a gun or a knife. It could have been a sling shot.

He didn't wait to find out. Slocum dived forward. His shoulder rammed into the man's rock-hard gut, driving him back into the crowd that was slowly forming in a ring around the fighters. Slocum and the man went down in a flailing pile, each struggling for dominance. Slocum staggered when a blow struck him on the side of the head. He wasn't even sure if it came from the Spider he fought.

New Orleans was the kind of town where an onlooker might have a bet placed and only wanted to change the odds in his favor.

"You're the other one," the Spider said, his pig eyes narrowed and glaring at Slocum. "You saved him back at the Web and now you're tryin' to rescue him again. Yellow Henry wants your balls, and I'm gonna give 'em to him on a silver platter!"

A thick-bladed Bowie knife came from the folds of the man's coat. He advanced with the tip toward Slocum in a way that showed long experience with knife fights.

"Get 'em," came the cry from the crowd. Slocum wasn't sure who was being cheered on. He fixed his eyes on the man's wrist, waiting to see the tendons tense for the killing thrust.

Slocum anticipated well, slipping to one side as the Spider lunged. Slocum got both hands wrapped around the brawny wrist and jerked with all his might. The knife went flying, and the man yelped in pain as bones snapped. Slocum followed him to the ground and kicked him in the side of the head.

The fight ended then and there.

There was only one problem. Davy Brookline had vamoosed again.

6

One problem had been solved. The Spider gang member lay unmoving on the ground, but Slocum looked up to see a half dozen others coming for him. One was dressed in a police uniform but walked shoulder to shoulder with the others of Yellow Henry's gang, which told Slocum he wouldn't find any sanctuary in the city jail.

Arrest by the New Orleans police would be as sure a death sentence as staying and fighting.

Slocum spun and dashed into a ratting parlor, ignoring the cashier's angry outcry that he should pay to get into the smoky, dimly lit establishment. Inside, a circle of men bet avidly on a rat fight. Two large dogs went after dozens of rats in a large pit that stretched from one side of the room to the other. Betting was brisk on which dog would kill the most rats in five minutes. From the knee-deep pile of torn, broken rat bodies, the count would be high.

"There 'e is! Git 'im!" came the cry from behind. The cashier at the door shouted obscenities when all the Spiders followed Slocum without paying.

They cut him off from easy escape.

Except for one way.

Slocum swallowed hard, closed his eyes for a moment and tried not to let his imagination run wild. Then he

51

jumped into the pit with the bull terriers and the horde of snapping, vicious black wharf rats the size of cats. Savage fangs ripped at his legs as he kicked and fought his way to the far side of the pit. The terriers took the diversion as an easy way to kill even more rats.

If Slocum got out of the pit alive, he promised to get himself one of the terriers. Now he was fighting to simply wade his way through the ankle-deep mud formed by dirt and blood. He got to the back of the pit where a ladder went up to ground level. Working hard, he kicked off the last of the clinging rats and scrambled up the ladder. Slocum ducked as a slug tore away part of the ladder.

Then he was out the back and running down an alley, trying to ignore the rat bites on his legs. His jeans were in tatters, but he counted himself lucky at having gotten away from two different packs of vicious animals.

"Where'd you go, you stupid son of a bitch?" Slocum wondered aloud about Davy Brookline. The man got himself into the damnedest situations and then slipped away with ease, leaving Slocum to get free the best way he could.

This caused Slocum to slow and finally stop to consider the situation. The Spiders wanted Davy's head, but Catherine's brother managed to evade them repeatedly, as if it were second nature to the drunkard. Maybe Slocum ought to let him go on his own. It seemed that the only time Yellow Henry's gang got close was when Slocum tried to help. It certainly wouldn't do for Slocum to be dodging shadows the rest of the time he was in New Orleans. The gangs ran the city. Getting one mad at him was no big thing since gang rivalry insured him safety in other parts of town. But all it took was one of Yellow Henry's men to spot him and he would die with his head caved in by an ax handle or a shining knife blade thrust between his ribs.

"I don't owe Catherine anything, and I sure as hell don't owe her brother a damn thing," Slocum groused. He came to a decision that didn't set well but was sensible—and safe.

Let Davy Brookline fend for himself. Slocum had done all he could to get the man to safety.

Making his way down side streets and avoiding the darker alleys, he headed back toward Congo Square and Catherine's fleabag hotel, which was not two dozen yards from the swamps. But Slocum's luck changed yet again, and he wasn't sure it was for the better. As he made his way west he came to a pier area where sternwheelers docked. At one ticket window, haggling with the clerk over the price of a ticket, stood Davy Brookline.

Slocum did not walk over to him and buffalo him to make it easier to drag the man to his sister's hotel. Instead, he warily surveyed the area, hunting for any sign of danger. Davy was a lightning rod for trouble, yet he always came through the storm unscathed. The way Slocum's legs ached from the rat bites convinced him that anyone around Davy Brookline would feel the full fury of the lightning.

Only when he was sure he was not walking into another trap did he slip his Colt Navy from its holster and walk slowly toward the man. Davy continued to argue with the ticket agent and did not see Slocum approaching.

". . . cain't *give* you the ticket. We don't need no more tinhorn gamblers on board the *Missouri Queen*," the agent stated flatly.

"I can enhance your revenue dis-distinctly," Davy said, still slurring his words from too much liquor. "Your esteemed captain will thank me when I split the take with him. Your line will make a fortune, all due to me."

"We tossed the las' gambler overboard. He was too much trouble," the agent said. "And you got the look of a card cheat. We don' want no card cheats on our boat."

"I—" began Davy. He cut off the sentence when he felt the cold muzzle of Slocum's six-shooter in the middle of his back. To keep Davy from running, Slocum grabbed his collar with his left hand.

"I think my friend's decided to work for a while to earn the fare," Slocum said, spinning Davy around and marching him off.

"You malign me, sir!" protested Davy Brookline. "I am a hardworking fellow, I am!"

"You murdered one of Yellow Henry's men in cold blood," Slocum said.

"Not so! I was celebrating, and he came in front of my, uh, celebratory device," Davy said.

"Your memory's improving. Before, you said you didn't even remember plugging Big Ed."

"Who *are* you?" Davy tried to wriggle free, but Slocum kept his hand on the man's collar, forcing him along the street, heading in the direction of the Regent Hotel. The mosquitos buzzed with increasing vitality and sucked at Slocum's blood. He swatted at them but worried more about Davy bolting and running again. The man was quite a jackrabbit.

"I told you before. I'm a friend of your sister's."

"Ah, yes, another of Catherine's paramours. I must say she got herself a real cowboy this time. I remember now. On Canal Street. There was some fight and—"

"Yellow Henry's men found you and tried to kill you," Slocum said angrily. "I saved your hide then. Fact is, I've saved it more than once tonight, and I'm beginning to wonder if it was worth it."

Davy walked along briskly enough, throwing off the effects of his heavy drinking with surprising speed. The hot, humid air wore on Slocum, and the insects all intently gnawed on his flesh. Nothing bothered Davy. He walked along and then began whistling a jaunty air.

"Where were you trying to go? St. Louis?" Slocum asked, remembering Catherine had said she wanted to go there with her brother to work in their uncle's mercantile store.

"Why not? It has been a spell since I saw that fair city."

"Catherine said she was meeting you there."

"That so? It might be true. I can't remember that little detail at the moment. Given enough time to sober up all the way, perhaps it would come back to me."

Slocum shook his head in disgust. Davy Brookline was a complete wastrel, not worth the lead it would take to send him to the Promised Land. For two cents he ought to turn him over to Yellow Henry. He heaved a sigh and changed his mind. What he thought of Catherine's brother did not change the way he felt about her.

But this would be the end of the trail for them. After he delivered Davy to her, they would part company. Then Slocum could figure out how to persuade Mrs. Lily Langtry to go with him to the judge's command performance in the middle of nowhere.

They made their way through the dark, quiet, sultry streets. Davy stopped trying to bolt and run, and Slocum's mind turned to his own problems as they walked. Kidnapping Lily Langtry was out of the question. Judge Roy Bean would stretch his neck so fast for that indignity he wouldn't have time for a last request. Duping her seemed unlikely, considering how well her business manager protected her from her adoring public. Glencannon was no fool when it came to scams, Slocum thought. The man stood to make a lot of money off the songstress if she kept her schedule.

He made nothing if she sang in Langtry.

The problem of getting the woman across Texas to Langtry grew until it became well nigh an unscalable mountain. Then Slocum had to push this aside. The Regent Hotel, with its single gaslight burning in front, loomed through the darkness like an oasis of serenity.

From a few yards off came the sounds of swamp creatures. A gator roared and birds thrashed about in the dark. Otherwise, the night was filled only with the endless drone of insects searching for Slocum's blood.

"Inside," Slocum said, shoving Davy toward the steps. "You and your sister can reminisce about old times inside."

"You are a churlish dolt," Davy said, apparently over his drunk entirely now. Slocum didn't know how a man that tipsy could become this sober so fast. It had to be practice.

Davy straightened his filthy clothing and then climbed the steps to the hotel lobby with a dignity Slocum would have thought possible only by some British lord. He followed, feeling shabby in spite of them appearing to be two peas in a pod.

"Miss Brookline," he said to the clerk. "What room?"

"We don't allow no male visitors after seven o'clock," the clerk said, looking from Slocum to Davy and then back. "Certainly not a pair of 'em at the same time."

Slocum drew his Colt and laid it on the counter where the clerk could see it.

"I've had a hard night and don't cotton much to arguing right now."

"Room 217," the clerk said, swallowing hard at the sight of the six-shooter and Slocum's steely determination.

"Do you always bull your way through? I could have convinced him in a few minutes of pleasurable dialogue. He would have *thanked* us for giving the information we desired."

"Shut up," Slocum said, trailing behind Davy as they went up the steps and down the long narrow corridor to the rear of the hotel. A second staircase came up from behind the hotel. If Slocum had known it existed and had learned of Catherine's room earlier, they could have come up unseen. Why that seemed important to him he couldn't say.

He rapped twice on the door. Catherine opened it. For a moment she didn't recognize either of them. Then she let out a squeal of joy and threw her arms around Davy.

"You're safe! I was so worried. And John, you brought him to me. Thank you, thank you!"

"Mind if we come in?" Slocum asked. He looked up and

down the hall, growing uneasy. He had no reason for this but always heeded his sixth sense. It had kept him alive more than once in the past. During the war he had tried to analyze it, to pick apart the feelings and learn what it was that warned him of impending danger. He had given up, deciding it was enough to have the feeling. It no longer mattered to him why he sensed danger coming at him faster than a freight train, even before he could see it.

"Yes, yes, of course. Come on in," Catherine stepped back and let Slocum and her brother into the tiny room. Plaster cracked off the walls, and the rickety bed groaned when Davy sat heavily on it. The floorboards gave precariously under Slocum's weight, and the window stood partly open, jammed because the sash had broken. He went to the table beside the bed with a small wash basin and jug.

Splashing water on himself got some of the grime off. He sank to the floor and peeled back his blood-soaked pants legs and dabbed at the rat bites. If any of the ferocious creatures had been rabid, he was a goner, unless he wanted to sail for France and take the cure with a man named Pasteur he had heard about. Slocum was no expert but thought the wounds were clean.

"Why did you leave Fort Worth?" asked Catherine. "I was going to catch up with you there so we could go to St. Louis."

"Saint Loo?" drawled Davy. "Don't remember saying we'd go there, but it looks like a good idea now that New Orleans is so . . . hot."

"Hot? Why, yes, of course it is," Catherine said, not understanding his meaning. "It's summertime."

"Ah, my ever-naive sister," Davy said.

Slocum got to his feet and stretched his legs. His ankles had been protected by the high tops of his boots, but just above the leather was where the rats had momentarily dined on him. He walked with a slight limp but was all right otherwise.

"Reckon it's time for me to go." Slocum touched the brim of his hat to Catherine, glared at Davy and went to the door.

"John, wait. We—" Catherine never got any further. Slocum had his hand on the doorknob but had not turned it when the door came crashing down on top of him.

"There's the varmint," came a gruff voice. Slocum grunted as feet pounded on the door, pinning him to the floor. Rolling, he finally got free and saw that three of the Spiders had Davy backed into the far corner of the room. Another held Catherine and leered at her.

He didn't know how they had found them. Probably the room clerk was in Yellow Henry's pay. If they had followed Slocum and Davy from the docks, they would have attacked long before now. Whatever the reason for being found, Slocum knew it didn't matter. The Spiders were in the room and willing to kill them all.

Slocum whipped out his six-gun and smashed it into the side of the man's head holding Catherine. Then he turned the six-shooter on the other three. He wasn't a back-shooter—and didn't have to be. One whirled about, a knife in his hand.

"Drop it," Slocum said. The words hardly cleared his mouth when the man tossed the knife underhanded. Catherine shoved him out of the way as the knife embedded itself in the wall. Slocum fired, winging the man and getting the other two's attention.

This gave Davy time to crash through the window and fall heavily to the swampy ground outside. Slocum cursed the man for not staying to fight, but it was all he expected from him. Slocum fired twice more, both slugs burying themselves in the closer man's belly. He doubled up and blocked the third man's attack long enough for Slocum and Catherine to stumble into the corridor.

"Down the back stairs," he ordered her. "Find your brother. He'll probably head for the docks. He tried to buy a ticket to St. Louis."

"What about you, John? I can't leave you."

His six-shooter blared again, forcing the third man back into the room. Angry argument told him the first man wasn't out of action any longer. Slocum joined Catherine taking the stairs down to the rear of the hotel. A buggy with a horse hitched was too good to pass up.

"Get in," Slocum shouted. He grabbed the reins and whipped the horse, getting it moving toward the docks. A shot from behind went wild, and then Slocum took a corner so fast the buggy almost overturned. They made a long stretch at full speed, another turn and another, and then he slowed their breakneck pace.

"What happened, John? Who *were* those men?"

"They want your brother for killing one of their gang."

"What?"

"Never mind. We have to find Davy and get the hell out of New Orleans or we'll all wind up dead. The clerk must have let Yellow Henry know where we were."

"Yellow Henry? What's going on?"

Slocum looked at her. Catherine's dark hair vanished in the night, leaving her face like a pale, ghostly oval floating in darkness. She was distraught and had every right to be.

"Your brother's brought down a world of trouble on your head because he killed a man in a saloon earlier tonight."

"Davy? He's not the kind to do that. This man must have deserved it!" Catherine maintained, staunchly defending her kin.

"Probably, but I've heard the Spiders are a gang that avenges every death." Slocum guided the buggy through the tangle of back streets, wondering whose rig this was. The horse pranced along sprightly enough, not caring who rode in the buggy.

"There's a ticket agent," Catherine said, her hand on Slocum's arm. "But I don't see Davy. Is there another?"

"There are agents up and down the dock," Slocum said, "but your brother's flat broke and isn't going to buy his way onto a riverboat." He reined back and jumped from the buggy. "I've got the idea he'll try to stow away since he can't buy a ticket."

"Now *that* sounds like Davy," Catherine said. "Always cutting corners and looking for the easy way out."

"Stay here while I hunt for him," Slocum said.

"I want to come with you." Before he could argue, Catherine jumped down to stand beside him. "Besides, this gang will be looking for the buggy. It would not do for me to stay with it." She shuddered as she finished her argument. "I don't *ever* want to ever again see that ruffian who grabbed me back in the hotel."

"Come on, but stay behind me," Slocum said. He prowled the docks, glad Catherine held her tongue. He was in no mood for chitchat as his anger at Davy Brookline grew. The man was nothing but trouble for everyone else.

"There, John, there he is! See him down by those bales?" Catherine gripped his arm, forcing him to look in the direction in which she pointed.

"That's him, all right," Slocum said. He took a step toward Catherine's brother, then froze. Three shadows moved behind Davy Brookline. Slocum swung around and clamped a hand over the woman's mouth to keep her from crying out.

Even if they had tried warning him, it would have been too late. The three Spiders grabbed Davy Brookline and began beating him with short wooden clubs.

Catherine struggled and got free. "We have to help him."

Slocum held her tightly. She saw six more men join the first three beating her brother. Together they carried the lifeless body to the edge of the dock and heaved Davy into the Mississippi. He hit the water with a loud splash. The Spiders laughed at their easy victory, congratulated one another and left to report to Yellow Henry.

Slocum and Catherine cautiously went to the river's edge. Drifting away into the strong current in the middle of the river floated a body, face down and unmoving. Catherine began crying softly and turned from the sight.

Slocum had no love for her brother, but no man deserved to end up in such a watery grave. He concentrated on comforting Catherine.

7

"Just like that, he's gone," Catherine said with a catch in her voice. She tried to turn toward the wide river, but Slocum took her shoulders and moved her away. There was no need torturing herself with the sight of her brother's corpse drifting where no man could ever claim it. The body might wash ashore downriver. More likely, the fish would eat it and the bones would sink to the bottom. Or a gator swimming out into the swift river would have a decent meal.

If eating a man like Davy Brookline could be called decent.

"He brought it down on his own head. He should never have killed the man in the saloon."

"That doesn't sound like Davy, but when he is drunk, I suppose anything is possible." She clung to Slocum and then pushed back. "What do we do now, John? I can't go to the hotel. Those men will be waiting."

"Maybe not," Slocum said, knowing she was probably right. Yellow Henry wasn't the kind of man who forgot a slight. And killing so many of his men and injuring others would not set well with him. He would want real vengeance, even if it included a woman.

More than this, Slocum didn't want to show his face

around town again. The clerk at the hotel knew him. So did the barkeep at the Web. Any number of others in Yellow Henry's gang had spotted him and branded him a killer. Slocum was as good as any man when it came to gunfighting. But he knew he had met his match going up against an entire gang—and an entire town. It was time to leave New Orleans.

But Judge Roy Bean still held his brother's watch hostage for Lily Langtry. Slocum considered following the English singer to Baton Rouge—or anywhere away from New Orleans. He needed to telegraph the judge in Langtry to let him know that his earlier entreaties either had not reached the Jersey Lily or had been ignored. Considering how eager her manager was to protect her from the public, Slocum thought the man might have taken the telegram and burned it.

"What else can we do, John?" Catherine asked, bringing his more immediate problem to the fore. "I can go anywhere. I suppose I can look for a job here. I know several trades that might be in demand, but if you have some other place to go . . ." Catherine let her words trail off, her meaning clear.

Slocum had thought they'd come to the end of their trail together. Catherine was hinting that it didn't have to stop quite yet. She had nowhere to go, no one to meet. And Slocum had a chore ahead of him that might require help, since it was so completely beyond his experience.

How would he convince a famous singer to go to the ends of the earth for nothing?

"Let's worry about that later. We can't return to the hotel, but I have a few dollars left from the reward. Another hotel, and one without a nosy room clerk, might be what we need to hide out for a spell."

"Hide out," Catherine muttered. "It's come to that?"

He said nothing as they made their way back to the buggy and got in. He wondered if it would be reported stolen. This was a fine horse and the buggy, while not of top quality, was sturdy and serviceable. He had his suspicions why it was parked behind the hotel. A whore plied her trade inside the hotel, and her customer made his way up the back steps unseen. Or perhaps it was a forbidden assignation. Quadroons met with wealthy men from the American Quarter in such surroundings.

"Where do we go, John?"

"Why not the best?" he said. "There's a place I saw down on Chartres that looked good." He drove carefully through the dock area and then faster when they approached the hotel. He left the buggy and horse a block from the hotel. He was filthy, and checking into a hotel with a woman and no baggage was not likely to go unnoticed. Slocum pulled twenty dollars in greenbacks from his pocket.

"Get us a room. When you've checked in, signal me and I'll sneak inside. They won't even let me in the lobby looking like I do."

As if for the first time, Catherine eyed him from head to toe and then laughed. "You *are* a sight, aren't you? And you stink!"

"Thanks," he said dryly, knowing she was right. Slocum waited for her to go to the lobby of the fancy hotel. He had no idea what story Catherine might tell to explain her lack of baggage, but it would not be too difficult for her, he reasoned. She was a lovely lady and obviously distraught. Around back, he waited in an alley by a locked rear door. It took Catherine only a few minutes to open it and let him inside.

"Third floor," she whispered. "Room 399, by the stairs."

In silence they made their way up the stairs. Slocum was relieved to see the room was at the top of the flight. He did not have to troop along the lavishly carpeted floor dripping bits of filth as he went. He slipped in, and Catherine closed and locked the door behind him.

Breathlessly, she said, "It was so much fun! I told the clerk the riverboat had lost my luggage and would deliver it by morning. I cried a little, and he believed me."

Slocum began stripping off the worst of his grimy clothing, dropping shirt and boots and gun belt in the far corner, but wondering about his jeans. As he tried to figure what was the proper thing to do, he felt rather than saw Catherine come up behind him. Her arms circled his waist and then began unfastening the buttons on the front of his jeans.

Her hands did not leave as she worked open the fly. Instead, those nimble fingers wormed their way inside to find his burgeoning manhood.

"Don't start anything you don't want me to finish," he said as she stroked up and down his hardening length.

"I know exactly what I want, John. I need to thank you."

"There's no need to thank me."

"Then make love to me so I can forget what's happened!" Catherine cried.

Slocum turned and faced her. Tears ran delicately down her cheeks. He kissed them away. Then he kissed her lips. She responded fully, crushing herself against him. They turned and turned as if dancing to silent music and then fell to the soft feather mattress on the bed. Slocum wasn't sure how it happened, but the woman worked him out of his trousers. He kicked free and then began working on her more complicated clothing.

The buttons popped open one by one to reveal the sweet, white swell of her breasts. He lavished kisses on them and then pushed aside the unwanted dress to work lower across her naked belly with his mouth. Catherine moaned and sobbed and began moving beneath him, demanding more than she was getting.

They rolled over on the bed, letting her skin out of more of her dress. Naked to the waist, straddling his hips, she rose up on the bed. The dim light from outside the room turned her breasts to marble and her face into that of a goddess. But the warmth beneath his fingers as he stroked over her firm, young body was not that of marble. Catherine was alive and willing and wanting him as much as he did her.

The dark-haired seductress wiggled a bit more and got free of other clothing. Slocum felt his hardness engulfed by feminine warmth. He gasped and lifted his hips, trying to shove himself in even farther.

"No, John, not yet. Take it slow. I want this to last. Make me forget everything else that's happened tonight. You can do it. I know you can." Catherine sighed and then gasped as Slocum began rotating his hips, stirring himself around in her tightness.

He sat up and buried his face between her breasts. Kissing and licking, he pushed her backward on the bed until she lay flat on her back, legs up high in the air on either side of his body. Slowly at first, then with increasing speed, he moved in the soft, moist channel until they were both groaning in pleasure.

"Yes, John, yes, I—" Catherine cried out her pleasure as desire built within her. What had been a tight sheath all around Slocum before now felt like a squeezing velvet-gloved hand. He grunted and lost all control.

He moved faster, drove deeper, found the age-old rhythm of a man loving a woman. Catherine's legs kicked on either side of his thighs and then they both experienced the ultimate release of pleasure. Slocum pistoned to and fro a few more times, and then sank down and pulled Catherine over to him.

They lay together on the soft bed, saying nothing, each lost in a muzzy wonderland of unfocused thoughts.

Slocum awoke to the morning light angling in. Outside, New Orleans was crisp and clear, if already turning hot again. He looked out the window and then back at the bed where Catherine stirred. She sat up and smiled at him.

"You look sad, John. Is there a reason? Something I can do?" She let the covers drop to reveal her nakedness and moved suggestively on the bed.

"I reckon so, but I wish you could help me solve a problem." He took a deep breath. There was no reason to burden her with his problems. She had watched her own brother die the night before, but she was resilient and seemed to take it well.

"Anything, John. I thought you were heading here for some reason other than to accompany me. What is it?"

Slocum told her about his clash with Roy Bean and how he was supposed to bring Lily Langtry back west of the Pecos so the judge could hear the singer he had become enamored of.

"He must have a great hold over you. Why, with that reward money riding in your pocket, you could have gone anywhere. He must be mighty rich, too."

Slocum had left out the part of his brother's watch being under the judge's gavel if he did not return. It sounded trivial to him, but Catherine had understood there was a powerful hold right away. She saw clearly things others might never understand.

"I might help you," she said. "I intended to seek employment and work my way north. I've worked as a seamstress in my day. Why don't I apply for a position with Mrs. Langtry and talk with her? I might convince her that she should accompany you to this town named after her."

"Would you?"

"Is Langtry a prosperous town?"

Slocum laughed. Then he sobered a mite. "I don't doubt the judge is rolling in money. He fines danged near everyone passing through Langtry."

"Let me get dressed, and I'll see if Mrs. Langtry will speak with me," she said, slipping out of the bed. Then she stopped and looked coyly over her shoulder, batting her long eyelashes. "Of course, I don't have to go *right* away."

And she didn't.

Slocum cleaned himself up the best he could without leaving the room. He sat and then stood and paced nervously, wondering how long it might be until Catherine returned. She had left hours earlier. He could tell by the way the sun climbed in the sky, though it now struggled to peek through black-bellied storm clouds building over New Orleans. He wished he had his watch back so he could tell exactly how long Catherine had been gone.

He almost jumped out of his skin when the door opened and Catherine walked in.

She beamed. "Good news, John. I got the job!"

"And?" he asked. "What did she say about meeting me? If I can see her alone for a few minutes, I'm sure I can convince her that Judge Bean is sincere about wanting her to perform."

Catherine sniffed at him and then tipped her head to one side. "You're a bit gamy, but you'll pass muster. Let's go down to the lobby. She's waiting for us right now."

Slocum's eyes widened in surprise. This was the last thing in the world he had expected. He grabbed his hat and hurried to catch up with Catherine, who was already out in the hall and starting for the front staircase.

"How did you do it? What did you tell her?"

"I simply told her a friend wished to speak privately with her, without that horrid manager of hers you told me about. She wanted to get away from the theater, for a while at least."

"She's on her way to Baton Rouge. I don't know how many more performances she has here," Slocum said, his mind racing. At the foot of the staircase, he stopped and stared at the solemn lady sitting on a chesterfield at one side of the lobby. Well dressed, she looked a little different than Slocum had expected. Younger or smaller, perhaps. But he had only Roy Bean's bigger-than-life description to go by.

"Mrs. Langtry," he greeted. She hesitated and then turned to him and smiled.

"You must be Mr. Slocum. Catherine has spoken well of you. What is it you want from me?"

Slocum looked at Catherine and then, at her encouragement, sat next to Lily Langtry and put everything straight in his head before speaking. He launched into the request to come to Langtry and perform. The woman sat quietly, occasionally glancing at Catherine but always returning her attention to Slocum. When he finished his plea, she nodded slightly.

"It is a great honor to have an entire town named after me. Is Langtry a large place?"

"Not very," Slocum said, picturing the dilapidated buildings. "But the judge is sincere about his admiration for you. He is your number-one devotee."

"It is nice having a fan of such stature. Imagine, a judge."

"I know it's a great imposition to go back to Texas," Slocum said.

"Back?"

"You gave a performance in Houston recently," Slocum said. "The judge mentioned it."

"Ah, yes. I tried to forget that terrible place."

"I don't think you'd like Langtry much better. It's smaller."

"Perhaps I prefer a more intimate stage for my show," Mrs. Langtry said. "But I simply cannot leave my current tour. My manager says I have to be in St. Louis soon."

"I thought you were headed for Baton Rouge," said Slocum.

"Oh, I am," she said easily. "My western tour ends in St. Louis. That is the reason Miss Brookline approached me, offering to work as costumer for me in exchange for passage up the river to St. Louis."

"It would mean a great deal to Judge Bean if he could meet you. You wouldn't even have to put on a performance," Slocum said, feeling his watch slipping from his grasp. Lily Langtry was intent on completing her tour, and Slocum could not blame her. This was a crazy request he made of her on Judge Roy Bean's behalf.

"Very well," the woman said.

"Pardon?" Slocum stared at her. "What do you mean?"

"I'll go see the town named after me. I am sure your Judge Bean will be a splendid host."

"What about your manager? Won't he have something to say about the change in your schedule?"

"Mr. Kincannon does not run my life. I choose where to go and what to do. Life is too short to do anything less."

"Kincannon? I thought your manager's name was Glencannon."

"See? I have put the wretch out of my mind already," the woman said. "You will supply first-class passage, of course. If you agree to this small condition, then we can leave right away."

"I'll get the tickets on the train," Slocum said, stunned at the suddenness of Mrs. Langtry's acceptance. "I need to telegraph the judge and let him know we're coming so he can prepare a proper reception, and then we can leave."

"Miss Brookline, come along and see to my luggage. We shall meet you in one hour at the train depot, Mr. Slocum. Good day."

"Good day, Mrs. Langtry," Slocum said, shaking his head in wonder. If Davy Brookline had been a lodestone bringing nothing but woe to those around him, his sister was just the opposite.

8

Slocum sat and stared at Lily Langtry sitting across from him on the train to Fort Worth. Everything had fallen into his lap after Davy Brookline had died so suddenly in the Mississippi. Next to the Jersey Lily, Catherine kept up a running commentary about the dreary countryside, pointing out the most trivial things to the singer. Slocum could never have convinced Mrs. Langtry to accompany him if it had not been for Catherine. Getting past the English singer's manager would have proven impossible for him.

He turned and watched the hot Texas landscape slip past as they got closer and closer to Langtry. At Fort Worth, they would head south, angling over toward Del Rio. From there it would be an easy train trip into Langtry. Slocum wondered if he ought to retrieve the horses. It worried him that the swaybacked horse Bean had given him might be left in the stable. While the judge might not take note of losing the almost worthless horse in his joy to see Mrs. Lily Langtry, Slocum wasn't counting on it. Bean had a reputation for conniving.

Conviction for horse thieving might require an even more onerous task for Slocum to complete before being allowed to go on his way. He snorted in disgust thinking about the Law West of the Pecos. If he did not play his cards right, Roy Bean might hold him hostage for a long, long time. How many of those apparently loyal deputies carrying the shotguns and backing up the judge were similarly held in servitude? The town of Langtry might be worse than any antebellum Southern plantation with its slavery.

"I need to get off for a spell," Mrs. Langtry said.

"In the middle of the prairie? I don't think that's advisable," Slocum said. "The Comanche have been behaving pretty well after Quannah Parker surrendered, but there are bands of renegades on the range that don't cotton to any white man—or woman." He remembered too well his own trouble with Comancheros and their double-dealing ways. Slocum did not fault the Comanches for wanting to lift his scalp. If he had been similarly cheated, he would have felt the same way.

"I mean at Fort Worth. Perhaps we can stay the night rather than continuing on."

Slocum looked at Catherine, whose bright blue eyes flashed with sudden anger. She covered her outrage well, though, when she spoke in a soothing tone to the singer.

"Now, now, Mrs. Langtry, we don't need to do that, do we? It's best if we push on and get to your namesake town right away."

"A single night will not matter," the woman insisted, facing down Catherine. "Will it?" This came out with a steely edge to it. Slocum noticed the battle of wills between the two women and wondered what was going on. The tension eased when Catherine finally agreed.

"Very well. We can catch a train for Del Rio in the morning, can't we, John?"

"I'll look at the schedule, but it might be a day or two. That's not a big stopover, after all."

"That's all right. I can take in the sights of Fort Worth. Perhaps I could even find a place to . . . sing."

Again Slocum felt the tense undercurrent between Catherine and Lily Langtry. It didn't make any sense, but a day or two wasn't going to matter.

"I can find a decent hotel for you, I'm sure," Slocum said, worrying about how quickly his cash was vanishing. The Jersey Lily had champagne tastes, and he hardly had a beer bankroll. The money from stopping the Jackson Gang was almost gone, what with buying first-class railroad tickets, meals and incidentals for Mrs. Langtry.

"I'll check right away about train schedules," promised Catherine, still angry with the other woman and barely concealing it now. Mrs. Langtry smiled sweetly and went back to staring out the window at the Texas landscape rolling past.

When the train pulled into the Fort Worth depot, Slocum took Catherine aside.

"What's going on?" he asked.

"I don't know what you mean," she said, her lips pulled into a thin line and her eyes flashing fire.

"Don't go making her mad. Mrs. Langtry's going out to see the judge because it amuses her, not because it's good for her career. I don't reckon I'll ever understand why she chose to go to Langtry rather than Baton Rouge and the rest of her concert tour."

"She has her reasons, I am sure," Catherine said almost primly.

"You didn't lie to her about what is waiting for her in the judge's saloon, did you?"

"You provided ample doses of the truth in that respect, John. Now let me go. I don't want to spend any more time in this town than I have to." Catherine pulled free and hurried to the ticket agent, leaving Slocum to handle their baggage.

Slocum's and Catherine's amounted to hardly anything, but Mrs. Langtry had several large trunks. She had apologized for traveling light, having left most of her costumes in the care of her manager. If there had been even one more trunk, Slocum would have had to hire the entire train to lug about her clothing.

"Where you wantin' to go?" asked a young blond man. His sleeves were rolled up and sweat beaded on his forehead. Powerful arms were crossed over a broad chest. "I got a wagon that kin carry all that." He pointed to the mountain of trunks.

"What's a good hotel?" Slocum asked.

"The Peachtree's a good 'un," the young man said. He grinned when Mrs. Langtry came onto the railroad platform.

"My, my, such a reception party," the diva said, running her fingers over the man's biceps. "I do hope it's all for me."

The young man blushed at such attention and said, "Anything I kin do for ya, let me know."

"He is taking my baggage to the hotel, isn't he?" asked Lily Langtry.

"Reckon so. He seems a stout lad," Slocum said.

"Good. You can join me for dinner. This young Adonis and I will get along marvelously, I am sure." With that Lily Langtry and the cargo hauler set off for his wagon. He helped her into the drivers box and then easily lifted the heavy trunks and put them in the bed of his wagon.

Catherine returned, looking dour.

"We're stuck here for two days, thanks to her." She tossed her head in the direction of Mrs. Langtry, who was now laughing with the blond man.

"She's not complaining. No reason you should, either. I'm the one who has to pay the bills." Slocum tried to read Catherine's expression and failed.

"I'd better go with them," Catherine said. "To see that there is no problem at the hotel."

"The Peachtree," Slocum supplied. "I'll get the horses and see to it that they are loaded into a freight car when the train arrives." He took the railroad tickets from Catherine, now distracted by how Mrs. Langtry and the young man were getting on so famously. Slocum glanced at the date and then tucked the pasteboard tickets into his pocket.

"Yes, of course. Go on. We'll see you there later," Catherine said, distracted. She lifted her skirts and hurried to get into the wagon before it rattled off down the street. Slocum watched until it turned a corner and vanished. He frowned, wondering at the way Catherine was acting, and then decided it wasn't worth worrying over. Get Mrs. Langtry to perform for Roy Bean and his responsibility was at an end. That and nothing else, other than retrieving his watch, mattered.

Slocum set off for the livery stable, worrying more than ever about Catherine and Lily Langtry.

"She has a passel of fans, I'll say that for her," Slocum observed dryly. Lily Langtry had seen a steady procession of men going to her room, the blond cargo hauler being among the number several times. "Do you think she'll be ready to travel in an hour?"

"It depends how many men are waiting in the lobby," Catherine said bitterly. Slocum studied her. There hadn't been much secret that Mrs. Langtry enjoyed men's company. A lot. What puzzled him were the number of times the woman left to send telegrams. He wished he could have found out where those electric messages were being sent. It might have been to her manager, but Slocum got the feeling they were being sent to different places. Even Glencannon wouldn't move around that fast.

And if Lily Langtry had been sending the telegrams to him, her manager would have sprouted wings and been here in Fort Worth before the telegrapher finished the last click of Morse code. He had to be losing more money than Slocum was likely to see in a month of Sundays having his star traipsing across Texas, going to a miserable jerkwater town on the Mexican border.

"We can make Del Rio by this time day after tomorrow and then get on up to Langtry by midday," Slocum said.

"Good," came Catherine's surly response. She had been distant since starting the trip with Mrs. Langtry. Slocum put his hand on her shoulder and felt her tense up.

"There's no way she can ever replace you," he told her.

Catherine's mouth opened. She started to make a nasty retort, then she clamped her lips shut. Anger etched itself on every feature. She was restive and irritable, and Slocum was beyond figuring out what was going on in her pretty head.

"I'll see to her baggage. Maybe that will convince her it's time to go."

Catherine stormed off, leaving Slocum alone in the hotel lobby. He was happy that the end of the trip was in sight. He was running out of money keeping Lily Langtry in such a royal fashion, especially when he suspected many, if not all, of her visitors left her a present when they departed.

A present of money.

The blond cargo hauler struggled down the stairs lugging two trunks at the same time to impress Mrs. Langtry. Slocum sank into a chair and watched, not offering to help. That young man had gotten quite a workout these past two days, Slocum reflected. And most of it had nothing to do with hauling freight. If any of the men she had seen the past few days had gotten a free ride with the Jersey Lily, he was the one struggling with the heavy costume trunks.

"Mr. Slocum, so good to see you," chirped Mrs. Langtry, as if she had not laid eyes on him in a year. "Miss Brookline tells me it is time to press on. The stay in Fort Worth has been utterly delightful. I really must talk to my manager about arranging a performance or two here."

"What's Glencannon have to say about you vanishing on him like you did?" asked Slocum.

"Why, I have had no contact with him to find out. I really do not care."

"From the number of telegrams you sent, I thought you were in touch with him." Slocum eyed her. He was good at reading card players, telling when they were bluffing and when he ought to fold and let a stronger hand take the pot. The sudden urge to fold and go his own way hit him, watch or no.

"My fans. They are all over the world. I do try to keep in touch with them." Mrs. Langtry's face turned impassive, as if she held a bad hand and was bluffing her way through.

"I have a telegram of my own to send. Judge Bean will want to know when we're arriving in Langtry. Why don't you and Miss Brookline get on down to the railroad depot, and I'll join you there."

"A splendid idea. I feel the need to be on the road again. Traveling, that is. On the train." Acting as if she had given away a deep secret, the woman hurried from the hotel, leaving Slocum behind to settle the bill.

It took most of his remaining money, but he had enough to tell Judge Roy Bean they would be steaming into Langtry around noon the day after tomorrow.

The train out of Del Rio steamed along, heading for Langtry. For Slocum's taste it couldn't have come any sooner. Catherine Brookline had turned worse than surly when they stopped over in Del Rio. Lily Langtry had vanished for over an hour, and Catherine had become livid with rage. She was a pretty woman, but not when she got mad. Avoiding her after they got back on the train, Slocum had watched the two women, wondering what went on between them.

It seemed incredible to him that Catherine had simply waltzed into Lily Langtry's room in New Orleans, presenting herself as a costumer and had been hired on the spot. Still, there was a slim chance it had worked that way. What gnawed away at him more and more, though, was the way Mrs. Langtry had agreed to come halfway across the West to a nothing town simply on Catherine and Slocum's say-so.

The laudatory telegrams from Judge Roy Bean might have spurred her curiosity, but her manager had a tour to finish. Why had she simply walked out on Glencannon and joined Slocum and Catherine on what had to be a lark?

Slocum shrugged it off. He had seen the way the songstress reacted to fans, especially in Fort Worth. She needed them the way men needed air to breathe. The lure of a man so devoted to her that he had named his town after her might be enough to intrigue her.

"There, there it is," Slocum said, sticking his head out the window. He could hardly believe his eyes. He figured Bean would do something special for the arrival of the chanteuse, but he had not thought the judge would go this far.

The train screeched to a halt at the station.

"What's that terrible cacophony?" asked Mrs. Langtry.

"Reckon you're going to find out pretty quick," Slocum said. He helped her to the door of the car and opened it so she could step out on the small platform.

From beside him, he heard Catherine mutter, "Oh, my God!"

He had to agree.

An eight-piece brass band played a song so badly he could not recognize it. Standing in front of the off-key band in a gray morning coat and tall black silk top hat was the Law West of the Pecos himself. A huge grin split his face as Judge Roy Bean bellowed over the loud band, "Welcome to Langtry, Mrs. Langtry!"

9

"You are most welcome," Judge Roy Bean said, pouring another drink of whiskey into an elegant crystal wine goblet for Mrs. Langtry. The woman took it and sniffed delicately at it. Slocum wondered if the rotgut had ever been within a hundred miles of Kentucky, as it said on the label. The rest of Bean's firewater was mixed up out back of the Jersey Lily, since the fumes had set the place on fire a couple times. Or so said the barkeep.

"They are hitting it off so well," said Catherine, as relaxed and smiling as Slocum had seen her since Fort Worth. "I can hardly wait to see . . ."

"See what?" Slocum asked when the woman's sentence trailed off.

"Why, the performance, of course," Catherine finished, somewhat lamely from the sound of it. Slocum had the feeling more was going on than he knew—or wanted to know. He had brought Mrs. Langtry for a visit, and that was that. Getting his watch back so he could drift on was of primary importance to him. Roy Bean was happy at the moment, but the mercurial judge could easily decide to feed everyone taller than he was to the bear at any moment.

Slocum wanted out of Langtry, Texas, as fast as his horse would take him.

"I need to talk to the judge," Slocum said, excusing himself. Catherine grabbed his arm and tried to hold him back.

"Let them get to know one another," she said. "There'll be time for you to collect your bounty."

Slocum snorted in disdain. Bounty? All he wanted was his rightful property. Nothing more. It had not been his fault he had ridden into this Godforsaken jerkwater town. But he wasn't going to let the judge do him out of his watch.

Not after all he had been through getting Mrs. Lily Langtry here.

"The time's now," he said. Slocum saw the flash of irritation on Catherine's face as he pulled free. He had thought on asking if she'd travel north with him, but that got pushed aside as he went to where Bean sat with his inamorata.

"Hey, Slocum, have a drink with us. You done good, my friend. I reckon I won't feed you to Bob after all." Roy Bean laughed at this as he raised his goblet of whiskey. The swig he took wasn't genteel. He drained it and had it immediately filled by the ever attentive barkeep.

"Glad things are going so good, Judge," Slocum said. "How about settling accounts so I can be on my way?"

"My, Mr. Slocum, always the direct approach," chided Mrs. Langtry. She laughed and laid her hand on Bean's arm. The man beamed as if the sun had poked its face through storm clouds.

"Later, Slocum. I'll see you get what you're anglin' for later."

"You said—"

"Later." The sharpness in Bean's order set Slocum's teeth on edge. He had feared he would be played for a fool, danced around like the judge's pet bear.

"Later," Slocum said, equally cold. Bean glanced at him and then turned back to Lily Langtry, a new wild and improbable tale welling up from the man's fertile imagination.

"John, come on," urged Catherine, taking his arm and

steering him out of the saloon. The Jersey Lily was in the Jersey Lily Saloon and holding court like a queen. There wouldn't be any way in hell Slocum could get a thing out of Judge Roy Bean until the man decided he was ready.

In the hot afternoon Texas sun, they walked along Langtry's main street. The few buildings looked even shabbier after the fancy wrought iron and combination of Spanish and French architecture in New Orleans. The only benefit of being in Langtry rather than in the Crescent City was the lack of gang members hot for his blood. Leaving Yellow Henry and the Spiders behind had been as worthwhile as getting Lily Langtry to agree to come to this hellhole on the Mexican border.

"How'd you do it?" Slocum asked suddenly.

"Whatever do you mean, John?" Catherine looked wide-eyed at him, all innocent and pretending. "If you cannot remember, perhaps we ought to find a secluded spot where we can—"

"How'd you get Mrs. Langtry to agree to come here? And who's she sending all those telegrams to? She must have sent a dozen in Fort Worth and almost that many along the way. She sent two from Del Rio. One went to New Orleans. The other one?" Slocum shook his head. He had been trying to spy on her, but Mrs. Langtry had been too clever for him and masked the second address. There had not been time to get the telegrapher to tell him where the telegrams had been sent—or to whom.

"She is a very famous lady. I suppose she sends out information to her fans. Perhaps even to her manager. He was wroth when she said she was coming to Texas rather than continuing with her tour."

"Glencannon didn't seem the sort of man to roll over and play dead. She just walked out on him, didn't she?"

"Yes," Catherine said simply. The hot wind blew a strand of dark hair across her eyes. She idly pushed it away and turned to stare up at him, her blue eyes aglow. "Don't you think I can persuade anyone to do what I want?"

Slocum had no answer to that. The woman had talked him into doing things he would never have considered otherwise. He tried to get his thoughts in order. He had helped her, but they had met accidentally. After that, it had been coincidence they were going in the same direction. And she had helped him, after her brother had been murdered. Nothing smacked of her talking Slocum into doing anything he had not wanted to do.

Trying to rescue her ne'er-do-well brother had been the worst of it, and Slocum had gotten himself into most of that trouble with Yellow Henry and his gang of cutthroats.

A sudden gunshot caused Slocum to push Catherine to one side, draw his Colt Navy and whip around, ready to fight. He relaxed a mite when he saw Roy Bean outside the Jersey Lily, Mrs. Langtry at his side. The judge had a shotgun and was shooting at something on the far side of the saloon. When an anguished cry went out, Slocum tensed again.

"Stay here and I'll see what's going on."

Slocum hurried to the front of the saloon in time to see Roy Bean fire again at a man scuttling about on the ground like a snail in a puddle of saltwater.

"What are you doing?"

"Jist seein' how fast this varmint kin move, Slocum," answered Bean. He fired the second barrel of the shotgun. The man let out a yelp of pain. The judge had the gun loaded with salt. Every pellet of rock salt hitting the victim had to burn like fire.

Slocum saw that the judge was tormenting the man to impress Mrs. Langtry. What bothered Slocum most was that it worked. The woman moved ever closer to the judge, rubbing against him like a contented cat.

"I want my property back, Judge. I can move on when—"

"I told you, Slocum. Later. I don't like repeatin' myself. You got that clear in yer head?" Judge Roy Bean reloaded his shotgun, stuffing the salt down the barrel. He fired again at his prisoner. Slocum wondered what the manacled man's offense had been.

Probably nothing worse than having his horse go lame before he reached Langtry.

Slocum backed off, knowing the judge was likely to do anything he could to impress the songstress. This rankled. The judge had a vicious streak in him that Slocum knew could whip about like a sidewinder. Slocum didn't want to be around when the judge decided to bury his fangs in his leg.

Walking slowly back to where he had left Catherine, Slocum squinted hard. He thought he saw her standing in the doorway of an adobe house just off the main street. Slocum went to the house, but two men rudely pushed him aside.

"Wait your turn, partner," said one, fumbling in his jeans and pulling out a wad of crumpled greenbacks.

"Yeah," said the second man, a cowboy from the look of his clothes. "Somethin' this good don't come my way ever'day."

From inside the adobe house came the sounds of intense passion. In spite of the heat, Slocum went cold inside. Had it been Catherine he saw entering the hut? Or was it his imagination? He had to see.

"I want to see what's going on," he said. "You're not doing anything to that woman against her will."

The raucous laughter stopped him in his tracks.

"Against her will? She wants it, mister. We pay, she gives us what we want. It's that simple and has been since she got to town."

Slocum backed off, unsure of himself for the first time. Did he want to barge in and find it wasn't Catherine servicing every man in town with a few dollars clutched in his hand? Or was he afraid it was?

He went down the street, found a place in the shade and sat, watching the adobe. Sooner or later the woman inside had to come out. Catherine had vanished on him, but that didn't mean it was her inside acting like a cheap whore.

The sun dipped down over the Rio Grande, killing the intense summer heat with a suddenness that sent a shiver up his spine. But Slocum never budged from his post. Langtry came alive, with siesta time now over. Still no one left the adobe hut. Slocum noted that men no longer went in.

He cursed himself but had to find out. He went to the house, hesitated at the door, then opened it and went inside to confront Catherine—or whoever was entertaining all the menfolk in Langtry.

It took a few seconds for his eyes to adapt to the dimly lit interior.

Empty. The one-room house was empty.

He scratched his head in wonder and then began searching the place. He was a good lookout and had honed his skills during the war. No one had left—through the front door. It took Slocum only a few seconds to push aside a curtain and find a narrow slit in the back wall where an agile man—or woman—could leave without being seen from the street. In disgust he dropped the filthy cotton curtain and left.

He headed for the Jersey Lily in time to see Catherine coming out of the saloon.

"John, there you are!" she called, coming to him. She took his arm and clung to it. "You went to see the judge and then I lost you. What took you all that time?"

"Where'd you go?" asked Slocum. "You disappeared by the time I got back to the spot where I'd left you."

"Oh, I went to get out of the sun. And a generous young lady offered me some water. I talked with her a few minutes and then went back, but you had gone by then. Rather than fry in that horrible hot sun, I went back to the Jersey Lily."

Slocum said nothing. He might not have seen her if she had done as she said. Chances were against it.

"You're acting so strange, John. What's wrong?" Catherine's soft voice soothed him a mite.

"I want my watch back from the judge, that's all."

"A watch? That must be a very valuable watch for you to go to such trouble for Judge Bean."

"It's not worth anything except to me," Slocum said.

"A memento?"

"My brother's only legacy," Slocum said, not wanting to open old wounds. He still cursed the name of George Edward Pickett and his suicidal charge that had doomed so many brave men, Robert Slocum among them.

"I'm sure it will work out just fine," Catherine said. "Let's go back to the Jersey Lily. That's about the only place in town where there's any life."

Slocum let her lead him into the saloon. In one respect Catherine was right. Roy Bean had a monopoly on liquor in Langtry. Nary a drop was poured anywhere but in the Jersey Lily, all the profit going right into the judge's pocket. Bean and Lily Langtry sat at a big table smack in front of the stage where the judge intended for the singer to perform, but at the moment they drank. Heavily. It amazed Slocum that Lily Langtry matched Bean drink for drink and did not pass out. Even if that were the finest Kentucky bourbon, it still had the kick of a mule.

He and Catherine sank into a pair of empty chairs at the rear of the saloon. Slocum ordered and got an overpriced half bottle of whiskey. To his surprise, Catherine started in drinking before he could even pour a shot into his own glass. She knocked it back, licked her lips and then waited for him to pour a second.

"Good whiskey," she said.

"Didn't think you'd drink so fast," he said. "This is potent rotgut."

"Good," she said, draining the second glass and sitting back to let the alcohol work its numbing effect on her senses. "So many men in this town. Where are all the women?"

"Not in a saloon," Slocum said. "I heard someone say Bean's wife was dead, but he has three or four kids that help him run things. Don't know how old they are."

"Who's that?" Catherine asked when a man, better dressed than most, came in.

"Don't know anyone in Langtry, except the judge and his hungry bear." As if knowing he was being talked about, Bob roared from his place of honor in the far corner of the saloon.

Catherine laughed and then stood. "I think I want to make that man's acquaintance. He looks to be a successful rancher."

Before Slocum could say a word, Catherine joined the man, who might well have been a rancher, in a drink at the bar. Slocum felt abandoned, especially by the way Catherine ignored him when she spotted someone who probably had more than a few dollars jingling in his jeans.

He worked slowly on the remainder of his bottle, thinking things through and coming to no good conclusions. Too much went on with Catherine and Lily Langtry that he did not understand. The whiskey seemed to help deaden the questions he came up with—and the impact of the answers Slocum guessed at.

10

Slocum left the Jersey Lily while Bean and Lily Langtry were still sitting close together, swapping intimate lies and too many drinks. Slocum wondered how the woman could put away as much as an old-timer rum pot like Roy Bean, but then he decided it did not matter to him. He had come to a strange conclusion watching Catherine and the English singer in the saloon.

They had the air of soiled doves working the room, collecting as much money as they could off willing cowboys. Too much of everything that had happened from the minute Davy Brookline had drowned in the Mississippi River until now made little sense to Slocum. He wasn't too drunk to know that trying to figure it out would only drive him crazy. Accept what he could and to hell with the rest, no matter that his curiosity was getting the better of him.

He stepped out into the cold desert night and looked up at the stars. Hard points gleamed brightly, occasionally covered by wisps of high ice clouds that looked more like lizard skeletons than clouds. The moon wouldn't be up for an hour or so, leaving the dusty border town darker than a tomb but nowhere near as silent. The only real illumination came from kerosene lamps inside the Jersey Lily.

Slocum walked off and listened to the gaiety and then

wondered where Catherine had gone. She and the prosperous-looking cowboy had mingled with the crowd, dancing as the piano player hammered out off-key songs, and then both had slipped away unseen.

"To hell with them all," Slocum decided. He was drunk enough to be foolhardy but sober enough to know he dared not go too far in what he planned. He walked around the saloon, avoiding a man puking out his guts from the bad whiskey, and then went to a small, separate adobe building at the rear.

Judge Roy Bean's office.

Bean held court inside the saloon but kept what records and belongings he had here. Slocum tested the heavy lock on the door and saw it would take more force to break it than he wanted to use. Scouting the building led him to a water barrel at the side and then up to the roof. As strong as the door and lock were, the corner of the roof was weak.

Tearing at the wood and thatch, Slocum made a small hole in the roof and dropped into the judge's office. A kerosene lamp stood on the desk, but Slocum decided not to light it. The room was almost pitch black as he made his way around, more by feel than sight.

Sitting in the judge's creaky chair, he laid his hands flat on the paper-strewn desk.

"Where would you put it, you old horse turd?" Slocum wondered. He reached down and began opening drawers, rifling through them. The top one held a six-shooter and a box of ammunition, along with a few plugs of chewing tobacco and a collection of papers. Another drawer had what felt like a human scalp in it and nothing more. Slocum did not want to know. It wasn't his watch, and that was what he cared about most.

It took the better part of fifteen minutes to search the desk in the darkness. Nothing he touched felt metallic and round like a watch. He had studied Bean carefully all evening. The judge did not carry a watch of his own in his vest pocket. No watch meant he had hidden Slocum's away somewhere else.

"A lockbox?" Slocum expanded his search to a filing cabinet. All he found were messy stacks of papers. He finally conceded defeat and struck a lucifer, putting it to the kerosene lamp wick. The sudden flare of light blinded him. When his eyes adjusted, he looked around the room and shook his head in wonder.

He had searched the desk and cabinet. A quick glance in all those places again convinced him he had missed nothing. There was nothing else in the room that might hide his watch.

"Where'd you put it?" Slocum growled. He held the kerosene lamp high, mad enough to dash it against the cabinet and set fire to everything inside. That was the liquor talking. His more sober side forced him to set the lamp back on the desk and blow out the wick. He waited a few minutes until the wick had cooled off before restoring the glass chimney and then felt it to be sure it was cool to the touch. Slocum didn't doubt he had left ample evidence of his presence, but he didn't want Bean coming in and noticing a hot lamp and getting his suspicions aroused that way.

Slocum jumped up, grabbed the edge of the hole in the roof and pulled himself up awkwardly. The moon was poking up over the distant horizon and gave some light to work by as he replaced the thatch in the roof the best he could. It wasn't a good job, but the roof had not been in good repair when he started.

Jumping to the ground, Slocum dusted himself off and wandered around, hunting for some spot Roy Bean might consider secure. That would be where he would find his watch.

Slocum found nothing. Mad at himself for not turning up and stealing back the watch, he went to the stable where the swayback horse munched a mouthful of hay. Slocum threw himself into the straw in the next stall and rolled onto his side, shivering a little. He went to sleep after a while, with jumbled dreams of Catherine and Lily Langtry and his watch.

Slocum awoke and heard voices. He rubbed himself to get circulation back in his arms as he sat up. The swaybacked horse in the next stall whinnied loudly. He got to his feet and decided to feed the nag rather than letting Bean's stableboy do the chore. In spite of being so broke down, the horse was a determined beast and had carried Slocum a ways toward Fort Worth.

". . . a few dollars. That's all," carried through the stable door. "That's *all*?"

Slocum knew Catherine's voice when he heard it. He went to the door and peered around to see Lily Langtry and Catherine Brookline a few yards away. Mrs. Langtry handed Catherine a wad he thought was greenbacks, but he could not be sure.

"It's the best I can do. Have you sent the telegram yet?"

Catherine's reply was muffled as a horse galloped past. The cowboy riding it dropped to the ground and struck up a conversation with the two women. Slocum wasn't too surprised when Catherine took the young cowboy's arm and led him away, his horse trailing along behind. Mrs. Langtry watched them go, heaved a sigh that sent a flutter through the lace at her bosom and then headed in the direction of the saloon. Although it was hardly six in the morning, the Jersey Lily was already doing a brisk business, with men flocking in for their morning watering.

Slocum wondered what the two women had been talking about. However he turned it in his head, the phrase "thicker than thieves" kept coming up. He returned to the chore of feeding the other horses. There was no reason to do it other than because it was routine work he knew and could do automatically as he considered the snake pit he had fallen into.

Slocum's hand went for his Colt Navy when a shot rang

out. He spun around, hunting for trouble. It came from the Jersey Lily. Standing in front of the saloon, Judge Roy Bean bellowed out his message.

"All you good-for-nothing varmints, get your butts over here. If you want a ticket to hear the Jersey Lily sing tonight, you better pony up five dollars right now. There's not gonna be more 'n a hundred tickets sold since that's all the saloon'll hold without the walls fallin' down." Slocum watched and knew more than a hundred tickets were sold by the time he ambled over. Roy Bean presided over the sales with an eagle eye. If the barkeep had tried to steal even one thin dime, Bean would have taken off his head.

"Slocum, you gonna hear the lovely Mrs. Langtry sing this evening?"

"Don't have the admission price, Judge," Slocum said. "I spent all my money getting her here."

"So you did, so you did. Give the man a ticket, Charlie," Roy Bean said to the bartender. The man looked up in disbelief until Bean nudged him. "Go on!"

Slocum took the ticket and stared at it. Then he said, "I'd rather have my watch back, like you promised."

"Got to go, Slocum. See you this evenin'. Nine o'clock, when the sun's down and it gets cool. Court's in session!" yelled Bean, ignoring Slocum's request for the return of his watch.

It was what Slocum had suspected. He tucked the ticket away in his shirt pocket, wondering if a gun muzzle shoved into the judge's ear might spark his memory of where the watch had been put for safe keeping.

Glumly, Slocum doubted it. Bean was the kind of man who was so stubborn he would rather die than give in. Slocum considered forgetting the watch and getting out of Langtry while he was still alive and kicking, but then realized if Bean was a stubborn son of a bitch, then he was twice as stubborn.

•　　•　　•

It happened sometime after noon, when most of Langtry was taking a siesta and unsuccessfully trying to stay cool. Slocum heard the commotion and went to investigate, only to find that half the town was there ahead of him.

Catherine shouted and pointed at a man outside the small adobe house where he had suspected she had entertained most of the men in Langtry the night before.

"He tried to take advantage of me! He's a brute, a monster!"

The man growled like an animal and turned just enough so Slocum could see the nail marks on his cheek. Catherine had been close enough to leave her brand on his hide, and it made the man madder than a wet hen.

"She was tryin' to cheat me. I paid fair and square and she wouldn't—"

"Shut yer pie hole, you sorry son of a buck," shouted Roy Bean. The judge came out of the Jersey Lily, Mrs. Langtry on his arm. "You don't go 'round bad-mouthin' decent women in this here town."

"She took my money and—"

"I said to shut up!" bellowed Judge Roy Bean. He started to say something more, but Lily Langtry tugged on his arm and drew him close enough so she could whisper urgently to him. Bean shook his shaggy head and then settled down and began stroking his gray-shot beard. He squinted a mite as he stared at the man.

"Git your worthless bones into my courtroom," Bean said, leading the procession back into the saloon.

Slocum followed. He tried to get to Catherine to find out what had gone on, but he figured he already knew. She had taken money from the cowboy and tried to cheat him. The lovely woman was nothing more than a hooker, but there was nothing cheap about her. It disgusted him to think of Catherine that way, but everything she had done since coming to Langtry showed that she sold her body to the highest bidder.

Or any bidder.

"Git him on over here," said Judge Bean, pointing to a chair in front of the bar. Bean went behind the plank-over-barrels bar and leaned forward. He glared at the man held in the chair by two deputies.

"You been annoyin' a fine young lady."

"She's a damn whore!"

"Stuff a rag in it," Bean ordered. One deputy carried out the order, using a bar towel crammed into the man's mouth to shut off the flow of outrage. "I ought to hold you in contempt. I jist might 'fore this trial's over."

"Trial!" came the muffled shout around the bar towel in the man's mouth. Strong hands shoved him back down and even stronger ones shoved the towel deeper into his mouth until he gagged. The man subsided.

"That's better, you sorry son of a bitch," Roy Bean said. He picked up a gavel. "As I was sayin', you don't go bad-mouthin' no lady in *my* town. Yer a chicken-brained sorry excuse for a man, and I sentence you to . . . hang!"

This sentence brought forth a loud cheer from the assembled population of Langtry. Slocum tried to find Catherine in the crowd, but she had left. Mrs. Langtry whispered rapidly, but Judge Roy Bean motioned her away.

"The Jersey Lily herself's asked me fer clemency. Since she's a notable visitor and a lady of genteel manners, I'm reducin' yer sentence to tar 'n featherin'!"

This was met with even more cheering. The crowd surged forward and dragged the man out of the chair and the Jersey Lily into the hot noonday sun. Slocum was slow to follow. He had seen this before and didn't cotton much to it, but he wasn't going to stick out his neck to save the man. It might have been more appropriate to tar and feather Catherine Brookline, but Slocum wasn't going to make mention of that, either.

Not with Mrs. Lily Langtry doing all that whispering into the judge's willing ear.

Pots of tar were heated, and the sticky black pitch was dabbed onto the man. He screamed in pain as the burning hot tar seared his skin. Then a few chickens were brought over and plucked. The man was rolled in the feathers, coming up with more sand stuck to the tar than feathers.

"Now ride him on outta town, boys," ordered Bean. To the man with the hitching post shoved up against his crotch, Bean said, "Don't go showin' yer ugly face in *my* town again. Mrs. Langtry might not be here to plead for clemency for you, and I swear by God, I *will* stretch that scrawny neck of yers!"

A half dozen men hoisted the rail and bounced the man toward the far edge of town.

"Now, fer the rest of you brave men, come on back in and drink up. The lovely Mrs. Lily Langtry is gonna perform in a couple hours!"

Slocum had no choice but to join the rest of the crowd in the saloon. It would be a while before the Jersey Lily would grace the border town with her golden voice, but no one was going to complain to Judge Roy Bean about that.

"Make danged sure everyone's got a ticket, Charlie," Roy Bean told his barkeep. The man had a ticket punch and dutifully punched a hole in every ticket as the men crowded back into the Jersey Lily after the all-day drinking spree. Slocum was a bit woozy from the boozing, but somehow the edge had been taken off his anger. If anything, he was anxious to hear Lily Langtry perform. He wanted to know what so intrigued Roy Bean that he went to such lengths to get her here, much less name the town and his saloon after her.

The piano player started a tune, and then Bean roared for the crowd to get quiet.

"I'll feed the next one of you to my bear who makes any noise but applaudin' and cheerin'." Roy Bean looked around the room and not a soul there doubted him.

"That's better. Gents, here is the finest chanteuse in the whole wide world. I give you, straight from England, the land of them bastards we fought and won our independence from, none other than the original Jersey Lily, Mrs. Lily Langtry herself!" Bean turned and glared at the crowd. "Applaud, damn you all!"

The applause was deafening. Slocum found himself joining in. Strutting in from one side of the stage in an outfit that looked to be made almost entirely of feathers came Lily Langtry.

For a fleeting moment Slocum relived the afternoon activity of tarring and feathering and had to laugh. Lily Langtry's feathers were bigger but no less ridiculous. Luckily, his chuckle was covered by the tumult spurred on by Roy Bean.

The woman began singing as soon as the piano player got to playing as hard as he could. She had quite a strong voice and belted out song after song, but Slocum found himself getting edgy from the screeching. For his money, and he had not paid for the five-dollar ticket, Lily Langtry was a terrible singer. Slocum worried that the town dogs might be running for the hills, their sensitive ears assaulted by the caterwauling.

But if any of the others in the Jersey Lily thought the woman's singing was bad, none showed it. Bean stood at the edge of the stage, taking in every off-key and strained note as if angelic hosts were performing for him alone.

Slocum's attention drifted from the terrible singing to the side of the stage away from Roy Bean. Catherine Brookline stood there, arguing with Charlie. The barkeep reluctantly handed over a sheaf of greenbacks to her and only then did the lovely dark-haired woman smile and step back, swallowed immediately by the crowd.

Slocum considered asking her why Bean's bartender was giving her so much money, but he knew he'd never get an honest answer.

He endured another hour of the appallingly bad singing from the Jersey Lily herself and then drank himself into a stupor when Judge Roy Bean ordered a celebration to end all celebrations in honor of his favorite diva.

11

Slocum saw it would do no good talking to Judge Roy Bean after the show. The man was completely wrapped up in lavishing Mrs. Lily Langtry with gifts and praise. More than this, Bean had been drinking heavily all day, and now that the performance was over, he was buying whiskey for everyone in the saloon.

Turning glum did Slocum no good. He slipped from the Jersey Lily and stepped into the cold desert night. Searching Bean's office had gotten him nowhere. Try as he might he could not think of a place where the judge might have hidden the watch. Slocum vowed to ask Bean about it again, first thing in the morning.

If Roy Bean did not deliver, Slocum was prepared to take the consequences for killing yet another judge. The one back in Calhoun, Georgia, had crossed him. Now, he had delivered Lily Langtry as Bean had requested. It was only fair the judge give back the watch for services rendered.

"That's all? There has to be more," came Catherine's querulous voice. Slocum walked to the corner of the Jersey Lily and peered around. Catherine faced down Charlie the bartender, backing him up against the saloon wall and pinning him there with her finger. She poked him as she spoke.

"I want what's due me!"

"I cain't give what I don't have," Charlie whined.

"You know how much she gave up to make this appearance? A world tour! She gave it up to come hold hands with your justice of the peace. There's got to be more."

"The judge took a fair amount of it," Charlie complained. "For expenses. It costs a lot to serve up free whiskey to a saloon filled with so many dry mouths."

"I've drunk his whiskey," Catherine complained even more bitterly. "It's so terrible it shouldn't cost anything at all. What's he make it from, gunpowder and rusty nails?"

"Well, sure," Charlie admitted. "You don't know how hard it is gettin' rusty nails out here in the desert. And then there's the nitric acid he adds to give it some kick. That's got to be shipped in all the way from San Antone."

"Don't give me excuses. I want the money."

"You been cleanin' out most o' the boys in town. There ain't much left."

Slocum turned cold inside. His suspicions were right about Catherine and what she had been doing in Langtry. He never thought she was a whore until she slipped away with the men most likely to pay big money for her attention. Slocum wasn't sure if he ought to be thankful she'd never asked him for money. He had paid more than one soiled dove for her services in his day, but he had thought better of Catherine Brookline.

It might have been her brother's death that pushed her over the line, but he did not think so. She took to the life of a cyprian far too readily.

"I can make you real happy," Catherine said, no longer poking Charlie with her finger. She moved closer. Slocum couldn't see where she put her hand, but he could guess from the way Charlie reacted. "I can make you happy, and you can make me happy passing along that money."

"I would, Miss Brookline. I would if I had the money!" the barkeep cried. "But stealin' from the judge is a sure hangin' offense out here. He *owns* Langtry, lock, stock and barrel."

"Especially the barrels," Catherine said coldly, stepping away. "I'll talk to him—and Mrs. Langtry—about this."

"You do that," Charlie said, but he spoke to empty desert. Catherine had vanished like a ghost in the night.

Slocum returned to the stables and the swayback horse, who seemed his only friend in town. He tended to the animal, mucked the stall and thought this was about the cleanest, most honest work going on in Langtry. Then he worked on the paint he had bought in Abilene, but the horse was nowhere as appreciative as the swayback mare.

"Morning," he said to the old horse. "I'll get my watch in the morning, then I'll be out of here so fast you'll think you're watching a quarter horse." The swayback mare looked unimpressed and nickered. Slocum gave her a carrot and then flopped into the straw to sleep off the haze in his head from his all-day drinking bout.

"Judge," Slocum said, going to where Bean sat in the saloon, his chair rocked back to rest against the wall. "It's time for you to give the watch back. I've done what I was told to."

"Purty singin' last night, wasn't it?" Roy Bean said, looking dreamy. "She's one fine songstress. The best in the whole danged miserable world."

"The watch." Slocum squared off. He didn't want to throw down on the judge. He could not tell if Bean was packing an iron or not. The six-shooter might still be in the center drawer of the judge's office out back. It hardly mattered to him, though. He had reached the end of his patience.

Roy Bean squinted at him and shook his head sadly. "Don't go doin' anything yer likely to regret, Slocum," the man cautioned. Bean pointed. His two deputies sat at opposite corners of the saloon, shotguns laid across their laps. Slocum could see one had both hammers pulled back on his double-barreled cannon. He figured the other was ready for a showdown, too.

Caught in a crossfire from two scatter guns, Slocum would be blown into a gory rain of dismembered parts. There might not be enough left to sweep up and put in a coffin to bury over in the potter's field.

"I'm past caring about that, Judge," Slocum said. "I can get a shot off before either of your boys can lift their shotguns."

"You'll be dead," Bean pointed out.

"So'll you."

"Now, this here's what I call a Mexican standoff. You heard them stories 'bout the Alamo, how the brave Texicans held off Santy Anna's whole damn army, haven't you? The finest bunch of men ever to fight a war."

"The watch."

"You got a one-track mind, Slocum. Stubborn, too." Bean laughed. "Sorta like me."

Slocum said nothing, letting the judge think through his options. Slocum had no desire to die, but if it looked like either of the deputies so much as hiccuped, Slocum would make sure Judge Roy Bean died on the spot. His determination was obvious to the self-styled Law West of the Pecos.

"You only heard the part of the sentence you wanted to hear, Slocum," Bean said.

"There's more? All you asked me to do was ride that swaybacked horse to fetch Mrs. Langtry. I did that for you, although she hadn't received any of your telegrams."

"Now that's a damn lie!" flared Bean. "She tole me she got 'em all, and that's what persuaded her to come out here. You wasn't more than a travelin' companion for her. You took real good care of her, and fer that I'll forgive you fer lyin'."

Slocum held his tongue now. He wasn't used to lengthy argument, not like Roy Bean. The man seemed to be as happy as a hog in a wallow now, enjoying the debate. Slocum had to tell himself the man was a lawyer and used to presenting cases in court, although he doubted any jury in this town ever went against Bean's verdict.

"Yes, sir, Slocum, you done good bringin' me the lovely Mrs. Lily Langtry."

"It cost me well nigh three hundred dollars putting her up in a fancy hotel in Fort Worth and buying first-class railroad tickets."

"I thank you for that, too," Bean went on. Slocum didn't hear even a hint of an offer to repay him. "But I want to know about that horse I loaned you. You didn't go and leave a valuable animal like her out there on the prairie, now did you?"

"That hay burner's in the stable. I brought her back in better condition than I got her in." Slocum saw the flash of consternation on Bean's face. He had hoped to use the loss of the horse as a lever to keep Slocum in town.

"Don't go annoyin' me, Slocum," Bean said crossly, "askin' for yer watch again. You ain't worked off the full sentence."

"Spell it out. Everything I have to do to get my watch back. And those two and the barkeep will be my witnesses."

Bean again showed a flash of anger, which then subsided. "Be like that. You'll git that danged watch back when you escort Mrs. Langtry to San Antone for her next performance."

"San Antonio? Why there?" Slocum had heard clearly she had been heading north, to Baton Rouge and then to St. Louis.

"Why, that's the next stop on her grand worldwide tour," Bean said, frowning. "She only made a small side trip to come to Langtry to meet me and sing in her namesake saloon."

"Mrs. Langtry told you that?" asked Slocum.

" 'Course she did. Now, what I want from you to finish

out yer sentence is to escort her to San Antone in time for her command performance."

"Then I get my watch?"

"You *are* a determined owlhoot, ain't you, Slocum?" Bean heaved a sigh and then said, "You git the damned watch back when Lily's in San Antone."

"You've still got it? If you don't, I'll—"

"Don't go threatenin' me, Slocum. I haven't adjourned court from the time I sentenced you. This here court's *always* in session, and I'd hate like hell to hold you in contempt."

Slocum said nothing about the contempt in which he held the pompous judge. He took a deep breath and then relaxed the set to his shoulders. He had witnesses, and Bean would lose face if he failed to deliver the watch after Slocum got Lily Langtry to San Antonio. He wondered, though, about the woman telling Bean this was a part of her scheduled tour. It might be she had used this as an easy excuse to get away from Langtry, Texas. Slocum was past caring what lies were being told and by whom.

"I'll see her to San Antonio, then I'll come right back. I expect my watch to be in good condition."

"It's runnin' jist fine, Slocum. Trust me."

"When is she planning on leaving?"

"Three days. A day or two travelin' on that good-for-nothing railroad and you'll be back to claim your watch in a week, your criminal record expunged." Bean looked proud of himself. "That's a legal term meanin' you don't have any charges that matter piled up ag'in you in my court."

"I'll expect you to buy us the tickets."

"I'll give you some money fer a decent trip. Cain't expect a lady to pay fer her own meals, either. And you said you done squandered all yer money."

Slocum left the Jersey Lily before he got mad all over again. As he passed the man with the shotgun nearest the door, he saw he had both hammers pulled back, too. There would have been four barrels of buckshot ripping him apart. For a brief instant he wondered if he ought not have thrown down on Bean and tried to get his watch back rather than agreeing to being Mrs. Langtry's nursemaid on yet another trip across Texas.

His belly growling, Slocum went to rustle up some grub. He had only a few dollars left, and the price on everything was high in Langtry, all the profits flowing directly into the judge's pocket, Slocum guessed. Hard tack and a can of beans looked mighty good to him as he went behind the stables and munched away, hardly tasting the food. A swallow or two of water helped the hard tack go down his throat and kill the sour taste to the beans, but it was better than what he was used to most of the time on the trail.

He was finishing his meal when gunshots sounded from the Jersey Lily. Slocum poked his head around the side of the stables to see Roy Bean standing in front of the saloon, a six-shooter in his hand. He was shooting lizards to impress Lily Langtry. The woman clapped and applauded and even kissed his bearded cheek as Bean polished off one lizard after another.

"Show-off," Slocum grumbled. Then he saw Catherine across the street. He felt a curious mix of emotions seeing her in the bright daylight. She was about the prettiest filly he had seen in years, but there was a rotten core to her that only showed up when money was mentioned. She hadn't seemed too upset over losing her brother, but Slocum could excuse that. Davy Brookline hadn't been much of a human being.

Only slowly had Slocum found out that the man's sister was hardly any better.

He watched her pacing back and forth, as if impatiently waiting for someone. Slocum stood and waited, wondering who she was meeting. A man came a few minutes later. Hardly anyone in Langtry looked to be anything but peon or cowboy—except this gent. He wore his six-gun down low, as if he fancied himself a gunfighter. There was a hardness to him that others in Langtry lacked.

Whatever went on between the two, Catherine more than held her own. As she had done with Charlie the barkeep, the dark-haired woman backed the gunman down. Slocum's curiosity got the best of him. He had to hear what was going on.

He circled the stables and came out on the other side in time to see Catherine and the rawboned man vanish behind the adobe building across the street. He hurried over, careful not to come on them unexpectedly. Every sense straining, he listened.

Smell told him the gunman was just around the corner.

Slocum waited a few seconds to be sure he wasn't mistaking a pile of rotting garbage for the man's ill-kept trail stench, and then he heard Catherine speaking, exasperation in her tone.

"Why not?" she demanded.

"You need to get more," the man answered.

Slocum chanced a quick glance around the corner. Catherine and the man stood a few yards away, their backs to him. He watched, wary of either turning to spy him. They stared out across the desolate desert surrounding Langtry, upwind and oblivious to his presence.

"Here, take this," Catherine said, passing over a small leather bag that appeared to be stuffed to the breaking point.

"This is all?"

"We're going to have to change our plans."

"It was too good to be true," the man said.

"The other plan—the one I telegraphed you about. We can try it." Catherine rubbed her hands together, as if trying to get blood off them. "It'll work out just fine. We need something more to pry loose some money. This will do it. I'm sure of it."

"If it don't work," the man said, "we'll all be in a world of trouble. And I ain't takin' the fall without draggin' you down with me."

"That's what I like about you, Utah," Catherine said sarcastically. "You're loyal to a fault. There's not going to be any trouble. It'll work. Just you get ready. When I signal, you move in."

"All right, if you say so, Catherine. Why can't this miserable jerkwater town have a bank to rob instead?"

"Because it *is* a jerkwater town, that's why," Catherine said, getting mad now. "You do your part, and it'll end up being better than sticking up a bank. Now get out of here. I've got work to do before you return."

The man Catherine had called Utah left without another word. Slocum ducked back and sauntered down the street, trying to look as if he didn't have a care in the world. But his heart nearly exploded when Catherine Brookline called to him.

"John. Oh, John!" she called.

He turned and faced her, expecting the worst, but she was all smiles.

"Buy a girl a drink?" Catherine locked her arm through his. "I need something to whet my whistle on a hot, dusty day like this."

"They're all hot and dusty in Langtry," Slocum said. Together he and Catherine went into the Jersey Lily. Never once did she mention talking to Utah and not once did Slocum ask.

12

"Have a drink, Slocum," urged Roy Bean. "Can't afford it, Judge. You don't pay me enough," Slocum said, pulling up a chair across the table from the portly man. "If I promise to deliver Mrs. Langtry safe and sound, will you give me my watch before I leave for San Antonio?"

"Now, Slocum, you know I can't do that. It's not legal. You got to do yer penitence 'fore I kin lift the sentence I put on yer head."

"I've come this far. I wouldn't desert her on the way to San Antonio. I might like to stay and listen to her performance there. With you keeping my watch, I'd have to miss out on that treat to fetch what's due me back here." Slocum couldn't bear the notion of listening to the woman's caterwauling a second time, but he knew this was one argument that might sway the judge.

It didn't work.

"She surely does warble like a songbird, don't she?" sighed Roy Bean. "Never heard anything so fine and pure of note in all my born days. Wish I was goin' 'long with you to San Antone. Wouldn't mind hearin' her all over again."

Slocum saw that the judge was changing the subject to

divert Slocum from recovering his watch. The best he could hope for was the man keeping his word. After delivering Lily Langtry to some unknown venue in San Antonio, Slocum would be a mite freer in what he could do to get back his watch if Bean tried to double-cross him.

For a moment, Slocum wondered what he was forgetting. Then he knew. Before they had left New Orleans, he had been taking Catherine into account on where he went and what he did. Now she was only an afterthought and not worth a minute of consideration. Seeing how she had sold herself to every man in Langtry hardened Slocum a tad more than he had been, and he had been a hard man before.

"Judge, I want to—" Slocum looked over his shoulder when Catherine came running into the Jersey Lily, shouting incoherently. He frowned when he saw her expression. When she realized he was studying her, that expression shifted subtly to one of horror and pain and even outrage. He had to admit she was one fine actress, better at this craft than Lily Langtry was at singing.

"Judge Bean, come quick. It's terrible, horrible. I can't believe it happened." Catherine put her hands on the table and panted harshly, out of breath from the running and shouting. She bent forward toward Bean just enough so the tops of her snowy white breasts were exposed to his lecherous view.

"Now, my dear, what kin I do fer you? Yer all sweatin' and out of sorts. A drink?"

"Judge," Catherine gasped out, her breasts rising and falling. "Judge, it's terrible. They took her. They took her!"

"What are you sayin'?" Roy Bean demanded. "Get a hold on yer emotions, woman, and tell me."

Slocum leaned back and watched, having the feeling he saw a carefully rehearsed play unfolding in front of him. Although he thought Catherine was overacting, his heart pounded faster. She still had that much effect on him. Worse, he had the sinking feeling that whatever she was about to say would involve him in ways he didn't want.

"They burst into her room and, and—" Catherine theatrically put her hand to her heaving bosom and straightened, as if forcing herself to calm so she could relate the awful news. "She's gone, Judge. She's gone!"

"Mrs. Langtry? What are you sayin'?" Judge Roy Bean's eyes flashed, and Slocum saw how the man came alive, looking a dozen years younger and more vital. The man was thrust into his element—and that meant trouble for someone.

Slocum hoped it would not be him but was cynical enough to believe that Catherine's scheme fell right on his shoulders.

"Yes, Judge, yes, yes! Mrs. Langtry has been kidnapped!"

"What varmints done this?" asked Bean in a deadly cold level voice that sent a chill up Slocum's spine. He had expected the man to rant and rave and carry on. Somehow this was worse. Here was the man who had conquered an entire border town and claimed it as his own. Here was an iron will and a stubborn determination that would see victory—or else.

"I don't know who they were," Catherine said. "They wore masks. There were three of them. She didn't have a chance. She was packing her trunk, and they burst in and gagged her. Mrs. Langtry fought. Oh, she fought them hard, but they were too strong for her."

"Did they tie her up?" asked Slocum.

"They gagged her and bound her wrists behind her ever so cruelly," Catherine said. The look she shot him was one of pure venom, as if she didn't want him interrupting her telling a tall tale.

"How'd they get her out of town?" Slocum wasn't going to let Catherine intimidate him. He was past being swayed by her charms, or even desiring them. Or so he told himself.

"Horses. They put her on horseback and rode out."

"Mighty hard if they tied her hands together behind her back," Slocum observed. "And she must have been wearing those big, crinkly skirts she favors. Riding in those would be hard, too."

"She did it," Catherine said angrily. She turned to Roy Bean in an attempt to shut up Slocum. "Judge, you have to help her. Don't let them steal away such a wonderful woman!"

Judge Roy Bean shot out of his chair, knocking it over. He stalked from the Jersey Lily and across the street to the house where Lily Langtry had been staying. It was a far cry from the fancy hotel in Fort Worth but was easily the nicest house in all of Langtry. Bean kicked in the door and roared inside, looking around.

Slocum and Catherine followed a few paces back. Slocum saw nothing inside to gainsay Catherine's telling of the kidnapping, but there was nothing to confirm it, either.

Bean whirled around and bellowed at the top of his lungs. "I'll string them owlhoots up and watch them kick their heels in empty air under the telegraph pole down by the undertaker's fer this crime!"

"Judge, look here," Catherine said, going to the bed. Both Bean and Slocum had missed a scrap of yellowed paper there. Bean snatched it from her and read it quickly, his lips moving as he went down line by line.

"Slocum, look at this." Bean thrust the paper at Slocum, who took it.

Slocum scanned the note and said, "A thousand dollars is a whale of a lot for ransom. Who has that kind of money?"

"Judge, *you* must have the money. Do as they request. Pay the ransom!" begged Catherine. She clung to his arm until he jerked free and began pacing. His earlier coldness had turned into prairie fire now. Slocum wasn't sure which he feared the most. Before, Bean's anger had been directed like a thin-bladed knife. Now it erupted like a sawed-off shotgun blast.

"Pay ransom!" Roy Bean lost his temper. He crashed around the room, smashing things as he went. He spun and faced Catherine. "I *never* pay extortion money. You give in to owlhoots like this and they never stop bleedin' you dry. It's their nature to come back and ask for even more money if you show any weakness."

"But they'll hurt her if you don't pay. They might even *kill* her!" cried Catherine.

"Millions for defense, not one cent for tribute!" bellowed Bean. "Those ain't my words, but they ought to be. I'm offerin' a *two* thousand dollar reward for her return—and the heads of them sidewinders."

"What?" Catherine stared aghast at Bean. "You're willing to give twice as much for a reward than the kidnappers asked for? That's crazy! Pay the ransom. Get Mrs. Langtry back safe and sound."

Slocum watched the byplay between the two and saw Catherine sliding down a slippery slope with Bean. The more she pleaded with him to pay the ransom, the more determined he became to bring his inamorata's kidnappers to justice—his Pecos brand of justice.

"My offer stands. Two thousand for them varmints dead and the *safe* return of Mrs. Lily Langtry!"

The words echoed in the small room and seemed to fill the streets of Langtry, Texas.

Slocum saw opportunity in the judge's obstinacy, especially when Catherine blanched and almost fainted dead away. She had never considered this reaction to her news. In a way, Slocum almost enjoyed seeing her discomfort at a plan gone awry.

"Charlie!" shouted Bean. "Get every man what kin ride out in front of the Jersey Lily in ten minutes. I got a speech to give." Roy Bean pushed past Slocum and Catherine, heading for the saloon. Slocum didn't see where Charlie had been lurking, but men began pouring into town like ants from an anthill.

"Looks like the judge has this under control. Anything else you can tell me about the gents who stole away Mrs. Langtry?" Slocum enjoyed needling Catherine, playing along with her scheme. She had to know he suspected her of being at the center of the plot to get the thousand dollars from the judge. No one else in this poverty-stricken town was likely to have that kind of money.

Slocum smiled wryly. After all, Catherine had picked clean every other man's pocket with her feminine wiles.

"You—" Catherine bit off her angry denunciation and stormed out. She headed for the edge of town, but Charlie grabbed her and forced her back toward the Jersey Lily where the judge had mounted a soapbox in front and was already haranguing the populace.

"We got a crisis on our hands, men," Bean said angrily. "I don't know who they are, but a trio of bandits has stolen away the Jersey Lily. For that gentle flower's return I'm offerin' two thousand dollars!"

There was moment of stunned silence, and then a loud cheer went up until Bean silenced it with the wave of a meaty hand.

"Miss Brookline's the only one what saw them mangy cayuses. Tell 'em in your own words, ma'am, what happened. I want every man here to know what to look for."

Slocum leaned against the cool adobe wall and listened to Catherine's halting description. It was even vaguer this time than it had been with Bean on the receiving end. She ended her stuttering recitation of the crime and hurriedly got off the box, letting Bean continue to whip the crowd into a lynch mob frenzy.

Slocum followed her as she made her way through the now-deserted streets of Langtry, heading for the northern outskirts. He had to stay well back because Catherine nervously looked over her shoulder many times to be certain no one trailed her. She was too agitated to spot Slocum, who easily avoided her inept attempts to throw off anyone trailing her.

She entered a burned-out adobe and, from all Slocum could tell, paced around in the ruin for a spell. He found a shady spot a dozen yards away that was out of sight and waited. Twenty minutes of patience on his part paid off.

"There you are!" shouted Catherine when the man she'd called Utah rode up. She didn't even give him time to dismount and go into the adobe to avoid being seen. She walked right up and lambasted him good.

"What's wrong?" Utah demanded. Slocum couldn't be sure but thought the man turned pale under his weathered complexion when Catherine told him. What he was positive about was the way the man's hand shook when he took off his wide-brimmed Mexican sombrero to wipe sweat from his forehead.

"You never said anything 'bout Bean actin' like this," Utah said. "He's got a reputation for bein'—"

"Shut up," Catherine said angrily. "Nothing's gone right. We have to figure out how to work this to our benefit. Get your ass in here and we'll talk it over." She turned and flounced into the burned-out building. Slocum took it into his head to leave, knowing they would be inside for a short time.

Hurrying back to the stables, he saddled the paint horse he bought in Abilene as well as Bean's swayback nag. If he had to, he could ride any man into the ground with two horses, one resting while he rode the other.

Even better, he could let Lily Langtry ride one while he rode the other away from her kidnappers.

Slocum made his way back to the adobe, assuring himself Bean was still haranguing the citizens of Langtry. He didn't want anyone interfering with his rescue, for that was exactly what Slocum knew this to be.

He got back in time to see Utah riding hell-for-leather from Langtry. Slocum angled away so Catherine wouldn't spot him and then found the fleeing gunman's trail with little trouble. Utah made no effort to hide his direction of travel, and all Slocum had to do was keep a sand dune between him and the other rider.

The sun began to set, and a nippy breeze kicked up off the desert. Slocum pressed on, determined not to lose

Utah's trail. The foothills turned into fair-sized mountains as Slocum entered Losier Canyon, much closer to Utah's heels than he preferred but not willing to let the other man get too far ahead.

Utah rode along oblivious to Slocum's pursuit. Slocum figured Catherine had put the fear into him when she told him Judge Roy Bean's reaction to kidnapping Lily Langtry. When Slocum heard other voices echoing down the canyon, he slowed and finally stopped, dismounting. He had not bothered switching to the swayback mare during the day, so she was fresh—or as fresh as the tired old animal ever could be.

"You're going to get a famous singer for a rider before sunup, 'less I miss my guess," Slocum said, patting the mare. He made sure both horses were tethered where they could crop at patches of juicy grass. Then he went exploring on foot, making his way carefully through the dense, tangled undergrowth.

He crouched when he spotted the kidnappers' campfire ahead. Working his way forward slowly, he took advantage of the now-sparse vegetation to spy on the trio.

The three men argued, none listening to the others. Utah waved his arms and his partners drew their six-shooters and brandished them. Slocum waited for gunplay, but it never came. He couldn't make out their angry, frightened words but caught the meaning.

Utah's partners wanted to leave, but he said something that settled them down a mite. They holstered their six-guns and poured more coffee from the boiling pot in the fire. The huddled together, as if this would hold back the avalanche of Judge Roy Bean's posse, and talked quietly.

Slocum took the chance to circle their camp, hunting for Mrs. Langtry. He worked his way around slowly, making as little noise as he could. He even startled a rabbit poking his head out from under a clump of prickly pear.

Then he spotted her.

The Jersey Lily sat in a sandy arroyo bottom a dozen

paces from camp, sheltered from the night by a mesquite tree. She hardly moved, making Slocum wonder if she had been injured. He didn't want to think of Bean's wrath if the kidnappers had harmed one hair on her head.

He moved closer and then stopped dead in his tracks, not sure of what he saw. Slocum was a decisive man—until now. If he made the wrong choice he might end up with a slug in his belly.

On the other hand, perhaps there was no right choice to be made at all.

13

Slocum flopped flat on his belly and simply stared at Lily Langtry. The best he could tell, she wasn't tied. The woman simply sat under the thorny branches and stared passively into the night. If she had been a captive, why wasn't she trying to escape while her captors palavered at their campfire some distance away? It might be that she was an English lady and English ladies didn't do such things as trying to escape.

Slocum didn't know. And what he didn't know in this instance might be deadly. There was no doubt in his mind that Catherine and Utah had conspired to kidnap her. Was the Jersey Lily a part of the scheme to bilk Judge Roy Bean out of money? Or was there something else that Slocum wasn't able to see in the dark?

He saw that her hands were free, but what of her ankles? Did her captors have her chained or otherwise tied down? If he tried to spirit her away and her ankles were secured, he would find himself shooting it out with three frightened men.

He kept coming back to the suspicion that Lily Langtry had gone along with Catherine's kidnapping plan.

"You all right over there?" called Utah. Slocum sank

down and pressed his entire body into the cold, rocky ground.

"I'm all right, no thanks to you," Lily said indignantly.

"You want coffee?"

"No," came the singer's ireful reply. She sat with her arms crossed over her abundant chest and stared out into the darkness. When she shifted her weight, Slocum saw that her ankles were unfettered. He had to make a decision soon, before the kidnappers figured out their best course of action was to kill her and hightail it out of west Texas.

Slithering like a snake, Slocum came within a few feet of the woman.

"Mrs. Langtry," Slocum called *sotto voce*. She jumped as if she'd been stuck by a needle.

"Mr. Slocum!"

"Quiet. I don't want them hearing us."

The Jersey Lily's eyes narrowed, and her lips curled up in a faint smile. Then she said, "I do declare. You've come to rescue me, haven't you?"

"The judge isn't going to pay the ransom. Instead, he put out an even bigger reward for their heads—separated from their bodies."

"What? He wouldn't pay to get me back? How outrageous of him!" Lily crossed her arms again, pushing up her bosom.

"Are you tied up?"

"Of course not. Where would I run?" she asked. Slocum had considered that. In her thick petticoats, the woman would never get very far before a cactus or thorn bush caught at the fabric and held her back. Moreover, she had no knowledge of the terrain, where to hide, or how to survive.

Slocum found himself tossed on the horns of a dilemma. It looked more and more as if the kidnapping had been done without her cooperation. She also appeared genuinely perplexed at the news that Roy Bean wasn't going to pay her ransom.

"Can you get away now without them seeing you?" Slocum asked.

"I can, but where would we go?"

"Back to Langtry and the judge," Slocum said. "There's a two-thousand-dollar reward for your return."

"So much for my return, but no ransom?" Lily turned this tidbit of information over in her head. "Roy is such a dear man." She pulled her skirts up and got to her hands and knees, scuttling toward Slocum. "However shall we escape? I cannot run in the dark."

"I've got a horse. You rode out, you can ride back. It's the gentlest mare you've ever seen," Slocum assured her. The swayback nag would hold the Jersey Lily better than it ever had held him.

"Will you receive the entire reward?" Lily asked as she came to sit beside him in the sandy ravine.

"Only if you get back in one piece," Slocum said. "And if those owlhoots are brought to justice, Roy Bean style."

Lily pursed her lips. "You mean the judge would hang them? Oh, my. I wouldn't want that. They haven't treated me badly."

"They kidnapped you. And they might have been planning on doing more than that," Slocum said, exasperated. "Come on. We can't sit here all night discussing it. We have to get away."

"Very well, Mr. Slocum. You are incredibly brave to do this for me. How did you happen across this camp? Even I do not know where they brought me."

Slocum did not answer. He was too busy finding a broad enough path through the vegetation for the woman to walk without catching her many layers of skirt on cactus spines. A few yards up the arroyo, he stopped and looked at her dress. It hung in tatters.

"You can't expect to get away and remain dressed like that."

"Do you intend to disrobe me, sir?" she asked, but there was an amused tone to her words.

Slocum reached down and grabbed a handful of crinoline and yanked. The haircloth petticoat pulled down the woman's slender legs easily. Seeing there were other petticoats remaining, Slocum kept yanking until a pile of fabric rose around the chanteuse's ankles.

"My, the night air is much colder than I thought, touching my bare legs and all," Lily said, sticking out an unclad leg so Slocum could see it.

"It'll get mighty hot if they catch us." He jerked his thumb back in the direction of the kidnappers' campsite. Slocum almost stumbled when Lily reached out and put her arms around him for support. For a moment, her body rubbed against his. He felt the corset stays and the rest of her undergarments. He also definitely felt womanly flesh and a completely uninhibited stage performer beneath the mountains of cloth.

"Perhaps I should shed the rest of my costume," Lily suggested. "I am so tightly bound inside, I feel as if I might explode at any instant. Do help me out, Mr. Slocum."

He hardly knew where to begin with the laces and stays. Lily guided him through the process of stripping off her unneeded garments. Within minutes, she stood clad only in the dress. The night breeze pressed it against her body. Slocum saw the ample swell of her breasts and the hard, taut nipples poking against the cloth.

"I feel as if I have been released from a prison. Thank you, John."

He looked at her sharply. She had never called him anything but Mr. Slocum before.

She laughed lightly. "Any man who undresses me so expertly ought to be called by his first name. You don't mind, do you, John?"

"Come on," Slocum said, unhappy with the woman. This hardly seemed the way a rescue ought to go. They made their way back to where he had tethered the two horses. The mare looked up with sadness in her eyes. It was time for her to carry a full load again on her swayed back.

"What a sorry-looking horse," Lily said, taking the rein and studying the mare.

"Get on. We've got to get out of here before they find you're gone."

"I had nowhere else to go," Lily said, finding her way into the saddle. Slocum watched to see if he ought to help the lady. She managed well enough on her own. Getting rid of the petticoats gave her the mobility to scramble around. Lily settled on the horse and followed Slocum into the darkness.

"Where are we going?" she asked after a ten-minute ride in silence. Slocum had been straining to hear any sound of pursuit. So far, so good.

"I'm not too familiar with the lay of the land around here," Slocum said. "We're traveling blind for the time being."

"You? Not familiar with the lay of the land? That's not what Catherine told me. She said you were quite familiar."

"You two are friends, aren't you?" Slocum asked. The question took Lily by surprise. He saw her turn her head to disguise her expression and take a few seconds to recover.

"We're as friendly as an employer can be with an employee. She's quite an outgoing girl, isn't she?"

"She's no girl," Slocum said, remembering the nights they'd spent together—and the way Catherine had gone after any cowboy in Langtry with two nickels to rub together.

Lily laughed. "You're quite right, John. She's no girl. She's quite the woman of the world."

"Quiet," Slocum said, reining back and holding up his hand to silence her. His sharp ears caught the crash of a horse through undergrowth a ways to his right. He had been lulled into thinking the three owlhoots were still in their camp. He had not asked Lily if there were more—or how expert they were at tracking. Slocum had followed Utah, but the man had been spooked and anxious to get back to his camp. That said nothing about how good Utah might be at following another man's spoor.

"What is it?"

"We've got company," he told her. His mind raced, trying to decide on their best course. Outracing their pursuit might be impossible. Lily rode easily enough now, but riding on an old, tired horse through the dark might be a different matter. He wanted to avoid a gunfight that no one could win.

"Dismount," Slocum said, coming to a quick decision. He hit the ground and handed her the reins. "Take the horses and go in that direction." He pointed away from the rider he had detected. "Keep going until you find a canyon wall and then wait for me."

Pulling the Winchester from the saddle sheath, he waited to see if Lily was going to argue. To his relief, she didn't. He watched her vanish into the night before heading toward the kidnapper he had heard. Carefully picking his way through the cactus and other spiny growth blocking his way, he came to a low rise. Crouching, he reached the top and peered over.

Two riders palavered. Slocum couldn't make out what they were saying or even who they might be. He sighted in the closer one, waiting for a shot. It might be a mistake knocking a man out of the saddle he did not know, but Slocum had Lily Langtry to consider, also, and she had been kidnapped.

He smiled to himself. Two thousand dollars in reward money from Judge Roy Bean wouldn't ride badly in his pocket, either. Bean had wanted the kidnappers brought in dead. If Slocum could do that, fine. If he could take them in for the judge to try and hang, Bean might like that even more.

Slocum's finger slipped back, then he eased off when his target's horse began crow-hopping. The rider fought to control his mount. Slocum considered his shot and then backed off. He didn't want to start a fight any more than he wanted the men on his trail. *If* they were even on his trail. They might be travelers with no knowledge at all of Lily Langtry or her abductors.

He hated doing it but had no choice. His finger slipped back, pulled smoothly on the trigger and got off a round that caught the rider's horse at the shoulder. The horse wheezed and died before it hit the ground. A quick levering action chambered a second round. Slocum's next target was bucking around, frightened. He still got a shot at a white V on the horse's chest, bringing it down, too. He hoped it died as fast as the first.

Shooting horses rankled him, but his life—and Lily's— might depend on putting these men afoot. If they were innocent range riders, too bad. They had escaped with their lives, which was better than a posse from Langtry might have allowed. Slocum slid back a few yards and then got to his feet and made his way toward the ominously dim, looming wall of Losier Canyon.

Before he reached the spot where he and Lily had parted, he doubled back, made a few attempts at obscuring the trail and then laid a false one making it appear he had headed deeper into the canyon rather than for the rim.

An hour of dissembling left Slocum tired and sore of foot. He angled toward the rocky wall, listening hard for any sound that might betray Lily's position. He had to admit that she had the common sense to stay quiet and not call out, even if he came close. Slocum finally found a fresh hoofprint in soft dirt and knew he was on the right track.

Fifteen minutes later he found her sitting on a rock, staring at the two horses eagerly gnawing at tough grass growing in a small patch. Not far away bubbled a small spring. She had done well picking a place to wait for him.

Slocum started to advance and then held back, staring at her. He had looked at Lily with different eyes before. She had always been overdressed in her frilly, full skirts and heavy theatrical makeup. Both were gone now, leaving a handsome woman. She showed none of the nervousness he

expected of an English lady abandoned in the American
Western wilderness.

He finally advanced. She heard him almost immediately
and twisted around. She had a rock clutched in her hand to
defend herself.

"Whoa," Slocum said. "I got rid of them, I think. For a
while."

"I heard two shots. What happened?"

"The men are on foot. I shot their horses out from under
them."

"The kidnappers?"

"That's why I shot their horses. I couldn't be sure in the
dark."

"A soft spot? I thought you were a killer, John."

"When I have to be," he said, not appreciating her words
at all. She implied that he was a soft man, incapable of
doing what was right. Then he got a bit confused.

She dropped the rock and came to him, her arms around
his neck. Lily kissed him hard on the lips, her passion un-
deniable.

"It is so scary out here, but not when I'm with you."

He found that words wouldn't come to his lips because
her hand grasped at his crotch, squeezing boldly and finding
that he was not a soft man at all.

"This isn't right," he said. "The judge wouldn't—"

"The judge wouldn't, and that was driving me crazy,
John. Will you? He'll never know."

Slocum wasn't sure who "he" was, Judge Roy Bean or
her husband. Lily had never mentioned him or why he
wasn't along with her on her tour. But he found his body
far ahead of his mind as he accepted her burning kisses and
didn't do much to stop her when she started unbuttoning
his shirt and jeans.

"Oh, my," she said, finishing with the final button. "So
much, and all for me!"

Lily dropped to her knees and kissed him where he was
most sensitive. Any rational thought now vanished as he

felt her wet kisses all over his manhood. Somehow they sank to the green turf, and Lily rearranged what remained of her skirts, swinging her leg over his body and straddling him. Slocum gasped when the woman wiggled about, getting his hardness into the moist channel of her femininity.

In the light of the stars, the Jersey Lily rose above Slocum, her breasts revealed. He reached up and cupped them in his hands. Then he squeezed. He was rewarded with a passionate moan from the woman's lips. She made better music now than in any of the songs she had sung back in the saloon. Slocum began massaging and stroking from the thick, broad bases to the lust-hardened, glowing pink nipples. He tweaked and turned them, spurring her on.

She began rising and dropping on his length, choosing the speed and penetration that excited her most.

"More, John, I want more."

Slocum wasn't sure how he could deliver more. She was in the saddle and riding high. He rose and circled her body, pulling her close. Her naked breasts rubbed against his chest. They kissed as she squatted over his lap.

Then she began rising and falling faster, twisting from side to side as she did so. The heat in Slocum's loins built, and he knew the woman's desires approached the breaking point, too, from the way she squeezed down so tightly on his hidden shaft.

"Yes, oh, nice, long, hot, so burning hot in me," she gasped and then soared past mere words. She worked her hips furiously, pumping up and down until Slocum could no longer stand the carnal heat ignited in his flesh. He exploded. Seconds later, Lily joined him in the land beyond pleasure.

She sank down and lay atop him on the hard, cold ground.

"I ought to be rescued more often. That was *exactly* what I needed, John. Thank you so much." She lightly kissed his lips and began working from his face to his ears.

"We ought to be on the lookout for the kidnappers. They

know we're out here somewhere and will want to recapture you."

"Yes," Lily said. She thrust her tongue wetly into his ear.

"They might stumble on us like this."

"Yes," Lily said, her trembling lips working down his chest.

"We have to be ready."

"You are," she said.

And he was.

14

Slocum lay alongside Lily Langtry and stared at her as she softly slept. The dawn poked gentle fingers above the canyon wall and small animals stirred, eating before the predators came out for their morning repast. Slocum knew how they felt. He should never have lingered with Lily. Getting out of the trap that was Losier Canyon ought to have been his only consideration.

She had beguiled him. But he thought he had come away a little wiser than he had been before.

She was a younger woman than he had first thought. The thick layers of theatrical makeup she habitually wore aged her considerably. She might be middle-aged, but Slocum doubted it now, seeing her in the soft, early morning light. In a few years, perhaps, but not now. Lily stirred and rolled over, muttering to herself in her sleep. She seemed so peaceful, so content, so lovely. For a moment Slocum saw in her what Judge Roy Bean must have noticed instinctively.

He disengaged his arm from around her. It felt like a dead log, her weight cutting off the circulation in it. She cooed to herself and tugged up the blanket to her chin. Without disturbing her further, Slocum stood and dressed quickly. The ground, even with the blanket he had thrown down, had been hard and cold. With the woman beside him, the edge had been taken off the chill but not the danger. The trio of men who had kidnapped her would be madder than wet hens. After all, he had shot two of their horses.

The more he thought about it, the more certain Slocum was that the pair he had fired on were Lily's kidnappers. This was an out-of-the-way spot, even for west Texas, which was noted for its long, desolate stretches of emptiness and sand and heat. With nowhere to go, they'd be on foot and waiting for him to ride past some spot they'd chosen for an ambush. Otherwise, they had to rely on the third man—Utah—to get them horses to escape what would be eventual death in this barren canyon.

Slocum hoped they had moved on, giving up on their ransom attempt. But he doubted it. Back in Langtry, Utah had been shaken by Catherine's news that Bean offered no ransom, only twice that in reward for Lily Langtry's safe return and the deaths of the men responsible for spiriting her away. Utah could be considering how easy it would be to turn in his partners and collect—if he had Lily back all safe and sound.

Even if they sought to double-cross each other, the three out in the canyon were dangerous.

"Ummm, morning, John. Sleep well? I did."

"The ground's a bit hard," he said.

"That wasn't all that was hard," Lily said, smiling broadly as she sat up. She showed no modesty at all. Her dress fell around her waist, baring her breasts. The cold morning air caused gooseflesh to ripple along them and her nipples to harden. Slocum took a deep breath. He had dallied long enough with her. Now he had to get to the bottom of this kidnapping.

If it even was a kidnapping.

"What's wrong? Don't you like them any more?" she teased, cupping her breasts and bouncing them gently. "You did last night."

"When do you have to be in San Antonio for your performance?"

"Oh, that? Soon, I suppose. I've lost track of time. That's so dreary. I enjoy performing, of course, but being with you is ever so much more thrilling. An audience of thousands is no match for just one fine performer like you."

"How'd you get out of your Baton Rouge contract?" Slocum watched the woman frown in puzzlement.

"You do go on, don't you? My manager handles that sort of thing."

"Who's your manager again?"

"Kilgallen, of course." A flash of panic crossed her features when she realized she had gotten the name wrong again, but she covered well. "It is so cold here. I could use a warming arm around my bare shoulders. And a hot kiss."

"Who are you?" he asked bluntly.

"Why, Lily Langtry, the Jersey Lily, of course. Silly man. Who else might I be?"

"I don't know," Slocum said, staring at her. His gaze cut through to the center of her being. She realized he wasn't going to be lied to any longer. She shrugged and began dressing.

"I told Catherine this would never work," the woman said. "For a while, though, I thought we could pull it off and nobody would be the wiser."

"Who are you?" Slocum repeated. "You're not Lily Langtry. You've never been within a thousand miles of England."

"That's true, but you *can* call me Lily. That's such a pretty name I think I'll adopt it as a stage name."

"You're an actress?" That explained her expert use of makeup and familiarity with other details of a theatrical nature. Those details had been used to enchant Roy Bean and convince him that she was used to walking the boards.

"An out-of-work one. Catherine came to me in New Orleans and offered me quite a lot of money if I pretended to be the Jersey Lily. It sounded like fun, and the money was more than I could have made performing in three plays."

"Who are the men out there? The ones who kidnapped you?"

"Oh, friends of mine I telegraphed from Fort Worth. I was born not far from Abilene, you see."

"Catherine really chewed out Utah."

"Utah gets—" Lily's eyes widened. "You know his name."

"I know the kidnapping was a sham to get money out of Bean. Catherine had already bilked most all the money from the other men in town, but unless I miss my guess, Roy Bean keeps his money pretty tightly locked up."

"He does," Lily sighed. "We could never find out where."

"Too bad," Slocum said. "He's got something that belongs to me. It's probably with his money."

"I'm sure he is quite rich. He owns that silly little town, after all, and bilks any traveler passing through. Like you." Lily laughed, a deep, rich sound that made Slocum feel better for some reason.

Slocum saddled the horses and made sure they were sufficiently watered. If they escaped out of the canyon without having to fight it out with Utah and his partners, it was still a ways back to Langtry. As he worked, he thought on the matter.

What was the point of returning a fraud to Bean? This wasn't Lily Langtry—not the real one. Bean wasn't the kind of man who would take kindly to being deceived. If he could, with a clear conscience, feed a man to a hungry bear for not paying a bogus fine, he was capable of actually stringing up anyone involved in duping him.

Slocum wondered if he would stop at hanging a woman. He looked over his shoulder as Lily was straightening what remained of her costume. The notion of him, Lily and Catherine all kicking at the air with a noose around their necks didn't sit well with him.

But he wasn't going to leave Langtry without his watch.

It was looking more and more like he would have to steal it away because of the way Bean refused to return it, no matter what service he did for the blustery judge.

Unless . . .

"That look on your face, John. I've seen it before on other men. What are you planning?" the woman asked. "I hope it includes me." Lily began folding the blankets, but Slocum saw how she watched him like a cat eyeing a mouse ready to make a dash for its hole. She was as much of a predator as Catherine Brookline.

"I don't have any love for Roy Bean," he said. "He's done me wrong, he's cheated me, and now he's started lying to me. What I'm proposing is a partnership."

"Sounds fine to me. We are certainly good together," she said with a gleam in her eye. "I'll enjoy working *closely* with you, whatever we decide."

"You were never kidnapped, were you?"

"No, but Utah and the other two cowboys with him aren't likely to split the take with you. There wasn't going to be that much, after Catherine took her share."

"How much did she want?"

"Half. That would have left $125 for each of us. Maybe we can figure a way of dealing Catherine out of the hand entirely and splitting the ransom money evenly. That'd give us each $200. I could convince Utah of that."

"Who is he? And the others?"

"Friends of mine. I told you that. Catherine didn't want me contacting anyone once we left New Orleans, but it'd been a spell since I was in this part of Texas, and I wanted to see them again. So I sent telegrams from Fort Worth and Del Rio letting Utah know where I was and when I'd get to Langtry." Lily smiled almost shyly when she said, "Utah was sweet on me. I reckon he still is."

"That's how you persuaded him to go along with the kidnapping?"

"He and his friends are cowboys. They don't know anything about being outlaws. Oh, they pretend, but it's all show."

"Just like you," Slocum said. He had already decided that about Utah and the way he wore his six-shooter slung low on his hip. Getting a six-gun out fast wasn't near as important as hitting what you aimed at with the first shot. Slocum had seen gunfights where both men exchanged a full six rounds and walked away unscathed. He had seen more than one where the draws looked to be dipped in molasses but a slug flew straight and true into a rival's heart.

"John, John, you're hurting my feelings. Not everything I do is play acting." Lily pouted, but the devil danced in her eyes. Slocum had no more time for what she offered so freely.

"Let's you and me and Utah and the other two talk turkey," Slocum said. "If you mean it about cutting out Catherine, I'm willing to go along to see what we can do."

"They won't cotton much to you trying to collect the entire reward, John," warned Lily. "You need me to go along, and if you hurt them, I'll tell Bean you were responsible for the kidnapping."

"We'll get the ransom money and leave it at that," Slocum said. They rode slowly back into the middle of the canyon, Slocum alert for any sound or movement in the undergrowth. They managed to get into the would-be kidnappers' camp before any of the three spotted them.

Lily rode in first. Utah jumped up and waved and shouted to her; the other two reacted more slowly. Then they saw Slocum and went for their guns.

"Wait! Don't shoot!" Lily cried. "He's agreed to throw in with us."

"We can't—" began Utah.

"He's not wanting to split with Catherine, just us. And he's not asking for half, either." Utah and his partners scowled as they worked out what their cut would become. Utah finally smiled at the number he came up with.

"Can we trust 'im?" he asked.

"Hell, no," Lily said, laughing. "But then, he can't trust us, either!"

"You shot two of our horses. You'll pay for 'em out of your cut," demanded Utah. The man shoved out his chin, as if daring Slocum to take a swing at him. Slocum dismounted, went to him and studied him for a moment. Then he thrust out his hand.

"Agreed. Shake on it."

Utah took his hand. For a moment, there was a struggle to gain supremacy, but Slocum allowed Utah to back off, content with a draw. He didn't care if the men took all the ransom—or the reward—money. He wanted his watch, and he was going to get it by hook or by crook. Bean had shown that he wasn't willing to return it. Slocum wasn't going to be any man's slave, much less Judge Roy Bean's.

"Have some coffee," said one of the men by the fire.

"We need to make a plan on how to get the ransom," Lily said.

Slocum sipped at the bitter, strong coffee while she and Utah shot back and forth with implausible schemes. Slocum listened with half an ear to their hare-brained plans, none of which would fool a sharp character like Bean for long. Slocum finally spoke up.

"Here's the way I see it," he began. In twenty minutes, Lily agreed. In thirty, the two men by the fire joined in. And in forty-five, Utah grudgingly nodded approval.

Slocum headed back for Langtry, leaving Lily with Utah and his partners.

15

Slocum rode back into Langtry, Texas, aware of eyes on him from all quarters. He tried not to look uncomfortable but found himself worrying that someone might level a rifle at his back and squeeze the trigger. He had no idea how much Judge Roy Bean had pumped up the hatred in this small, dusty town.

He breathed a sigh of relief when he got to the front door of the Jersey Lily and dismounted. From inside the saloon came angry sounds of a gavel rapping hard on the wood plank bar serving as Bean's judicial bench. Slocum went in, his throat parched and itching for a shot of whiskey.

"Ninety days or nine *hunnerd* dollars!" shouted Bean, rapping hard on the plank. Slocum saw he had forsaken his gavel in favor of the six-shooter that had been in his top desk drawer.

"You cain't do that!" protested the prisoner. From the cut of his clothes, he was a gambler who had been foolish enough to step off the train.

"You don't go swindlin' folks in *my* town," Bean roared. "If you don't shut that tater trap of yers, I'll toss you in the calaboose for a year!"

Two deputies swung the gambler around and grabbed him by the collar, pulling him from the Jersey Lily. Two more deputies stood beside a poor Mexican peasant who was nervously running his fingers around the brim of his sombrero.

"You not been payin' rent, ain't that so, Flaco?" demanded Bean.

"*Sí*, this is so. I have not worked because of my leg."

"Lemme see that gimpy leg," Bean said, peering over the plank bar as the peon raised a tattered linen pants leg. "Hmm, that don't look so good. What's the doc say about it?"

"I have no money."

"The hell you say!" roared Bean. "If that worthless sawbones don't treat you for free, I'll have him up on charges. And ferget the rent 'til you get back to work, Flaco." Bean turned his gimlet eye around and spotted Slocum.

"Get your ass over here, Slocum. What've you found?"

"I trailed them for a spell, but . . ." Slocum's mouth felt as if the entire west Texas desert had settled in it. Every bit of grit raked across his tongue as he prepared his lie.

"But nuthin'! You miserable cur! I'll have you horsewhipped and—"

"But I stopped when I got to the Rio Grande. They hightailed it into Mexico, Judge. That's out of your jurisdiction."

"I don't give a diddly damn! Fetch Mrs. Langtry back from those sons of bitches."

"The *Federales*," Slocum said vaguely, shrugging his shoulders. "They know about you and aren't inclined to cooperate, unless they—"

"Those bloodsucking thieves! They can't do this. A crime's been done!"

"Let me have a few dollars to grease their palms," Slocum said. "I know some folks across the river who can put me back on the trail. You really scared the kidnappers with talk of stringing them up rather than paying the ransom."

"They won't do nothin' rash, like killin' her, will they?" Bean peered at Slocum as if he could answer such a question. The judge's fingers ran up and down the length of the six-shooter he used as a gavel. He dropped the six-gun to the plank so hard it rattled, causing men in the room to jump. One deputy even turned pale with shock at the sudden sound.

"Time's not on our side, Judge," Slocum said.

"How much you need?"

"I can get by with five hundred dollars."

"Too much."

"But you'd pay two thousand for her return. If I get her back, take the five hundred out of the reward," Slocum said.

"If you don't rescue Mrs. Langtry, I'll take it out of yer good-for-nuthin' hide, Slocum. I swear, I'll smash that fancy watch of yers 'fore yer eyes. And then I'll hang you from the spout on the railroad water tower."

"I'll need some supplies, too," Slocum said, ignoring the threat. He had won his point. All Bean did now was rant and rave. "Getting over the river is going to take a while."

"Give this varmint what he needs," Bean ordered. "Get back on their trail 'fore sundown. I'm not a patient man."

"I'm not, either, when it comes to things like this," Slocum said, locking eyes with the grizzled justice of the peace.

"Git on outta here, Slocum. I got work to do, people to fine, outlaws to hang!"

Slocum left in a hurry, pleased with the way the confrontation had gone. He stepped out into the hot Texas sun and wiped sweat from his forehead. His plan had worked. So far.

Walking down the street to the railroad depot, Slocum went inside to talk to the telegraph agent. Langtry was so small that the man doubled as telegrapher and railroad stationmaster. The slight, drab man looked up as if Slocum had caught him at something illegal.

Everyone in Langtry was jumpy, thanks to Roy Bean.

"Howdy, mister," the telegrapher said. "What kin I do you out of?"

"I wanted to see some of the 'grams sent by Mrs. Langtry."

"What? I cain't do that. My files're private, not to be showed around to jist anybody."

"Judge Bean is mighty eager to get Mrs. Langtry back from her kidnappers," Slocum said, trying not to overplay his hand. "He might consider it a real favor if you'd let me see who she was sending telegrams to just before those owlhoots abducted her."

"How's it gonna help knowin' who *she* was sendin' telegrams to?"

"If I knew that, I wouldn't have to look," Slocum said. To his surprise the man bought the circular argument.

"Well, if the judge is wantin' you to see, I reckon it's all right. Here's my book."

He pushed across a thick bound book of flimsy yellow sheets. As he took down the incoming messages, he wrote them on a white sheet atop a sheet of carbon paper. The white copy went to the recipient and the telegrapher kept the copy. Slocum riffled through the thin sheets, finding only one telegram Lily had received.

He didn't recognize the name, but it was from a Frank Dupree in Abilene, confirming what she had said about her origins. This Dupree might well be Utah or one of the men riding with him. The telegram itself revealed nothing to Slocum.

"Thanks," Slocum said. Then he paused as a thought occurred to him. "These are the telegrams that came in. Where are the outgoing ones?"

"Here," the man said, licking his lips. Slocum realized he was pushing the man to the point of denying him everything—or going straight to Judge Roy Bean to find out if he had really sent Slocum over to paw through his precious files.

Slocum hurriedly leafed through the second book. Whoever sent a telegram handed the already-written message to the telegrapher, who copied it into this book for transmission in code.

Slocum found the original message Lily had sent that Frank Dupree had responded to. He also found a cryptic one sent by Catherine Brookline.

"What's this mean? Is something missing from it?" Slocum asked, holding up the book for the telegrapher to see.

"Oh, Miss Brookline sent that one to Del Rio. I ast about it, thinking she left out somethin'. She got real mad at me and told me to mind my own damn business."

The telegram said only: "D—Noon train fast." It had been signed "C—"

"Thanks," Slocum said, wondering what the telegram meant. He could always ask Catherine, but he didn't really want to have anything more to do with her. She had sent more than one telegram along the way from Fort Worth, and he had never figured out who might be receiving them. Now he knew.

"D," he mused. "Curious way to address someone." He shrugged it off as he went to get his supplies. The owner of the town's general store was reluctant to give Slocum any of the supplies he asked for on credit until Bean's deputy came over to ask Slocum why he wasn't back on the trail.

"Need some grub," Slocum said, jerking his thumb in the direction of the merchant. "And the money the judge promised."

"Here," the deputy said, handing Slocum a sheaf of greenbacks.

"What's this? I can't bribe *Federales* with scrip. I need gold. At least a bag of silver coins. They won't take this."

"I need to see what Judge Bean says," the deputy answered. He snatched the sheaf of bills from Slocum's grip and stalked off. But the brief exchange had loosened the merchant's notion of who ought to be given credit. He had everything he asked for waiting by the time Slocum turned back.

Slocum was loading his supplies behind his saddle when the whistle screeched loudly and huge puffs of white steam rose into the air, signaling the arrival of the train. Peering up into the sky, Slocum estimated it was not far off from noon. He sauntered back to the train depot as the engine grated to a halt amid a flare of sparks from the steel wheels sliding along the rails. The engineer was a good judge of braking distances and came to a halt directly under the water spout on the tank near the tracks.

"This the noon train?" Slocum called to the stationmaster. The colorless man's head bobbed up and down.

Slocum lounged against a post, watching to see if any passengers got off. The conductor jumped down, as did a hunched-over man dressed in grimy overalls. The conductor took a bag of mail from the telegrapher while the other man went to the water tower, grabbed a dangling rope and pulled the spout down to the top of the locomotive boiler.

The man worked to get the valve turned to refill the engine boiler.

"Jerkwater town," Slocum said. He turned his attention back to the passengers peering curiously from the train. Some looked downright hostile at having to stop. Others looked bored. No one seemed inclined to get off at Langtry.

"All 'board!" shouted the conductor. He heaved the bag of mail into the mail car and then hopped onto a platform between cars and looked to the engineer. The conductor waved his arm, signaling the engineer to get back under steam.

The engine quivered and belched and roared as the fireman began stoking the boiler with shovels of coal. The whistle screeched, and the locomotive began pulling the train forward.

"Hey," Slocum called, getting the stationmaster's attention. "The fellow who filled the boiler." Slocum pointed at the hunched-over man who had scrambled to close the valve. For some reason he jumped in front of the train as it pulled out.

"What?" The stationmaster-cum-telegrapher peered at Slocum.

The train pulled out, but Slocum didn't see the man on the far side of the track. He shrugged it off. He was getting spooked at the simplest things.

"Slocum! Slocum!"

Slocum turned when the deputy who had tried to foist the greenbacks on Slocum came up clumping the wood steps. The man puffed slightly from the exertion.

"Here's the money in silver, like you wanted. You better get results, or the judge's gonna be real pissed off."

Slocum weighed the bag of coins in his hand and then opened it and peered inside. Mostly silver five-peso coins, the money would suit him just fine. Let Bean think he was going to use the money to bribe lawmen—or bandidos— on the far side of the Rio Grande. This was going to be stashed where no one else could find it. Slocum wanted something out of this, especially if Bean made good on his threat to destroy his watch.

Five hundred dollars in silver was no replacement for the watch. But it would go a ways toward easing Slocum's loss, should it come to that.

"You fixin' to leave any time soon?" the deputy asked, his thumbs hooked into his gun belt. "The judge wants to know."

"Right away, pardner, right away," Slocum said, slapping the deputy on the back as he went down the steps and toward his heavily laden horse who was waiting patiently in front of the general store. Everything was going well, according to the plan he had mentally worked out on his way back into Langtry.

16

Slocum swung into the saddle. His sturdy paint horse complained a mite about the added weight of the supplies he had in his saddlebags, but Slocum knew the horse wouldn't have to bear it for long. He wasn't going into Mexico as he had told Roy Bean. Fact was, Slocum wasn't going far at all.

Just far enough to get his watch back.

He wheeled the horse around and was leaving Langtry when he spotted Catherine Brookline at the livery stable. She argued with the owner. That in itself wasn't too strange, but Slocum saw that she had two horses. The spat seemed over the price for two rather than one. Slocum knew better than to butt in but had to see what was being said. He headed down the side street for the livery.

Catherine heard him coming. When she saw him, she jumped as if she'd been stuck with a pin.

"John! I wasn't expecting to see you today." She looked guiltily at the horses, then to the livery owner and finally back at Slocum. He enjoyed her discomfort, though he wondered why she was buying two horses when neither was a pack animal.

"Afternoon," he greeted. "Looks like you're caught up in the middle of an argument. Can I help?"

"She wants to buy these here horses and not pay a decent price for 'em. I tole her these are the best I got," the stable owner complained. He calmed one horse trying to rear and lash out with its front hooves. Slocum saw that the horse didn't want to leave a stable with regular meals and a decent supply of water. "She says the judge wants her to have 'em at a discounted price."

"That so?" Slocum said neutrally. He watched lovely, dark-haired Catherine, trying to read her as he would someone sitting across a poker table from him. What he saw made no sense. She was upset, but over him finding her at the purchase or over the purchase of two horses itself? He couldn't tell.

And it didn't much matter to him.

"I *think* the judge would approve," Catherine hedged.

"You can always go ask him. He's over at the Jersey Lily holding court," Slocum said, enjoying the way the woman squirmed. "I've got to get back on the trail."

"Have you found Mrs. Langtry?" Catherine asked quickly, betraying her concern by asking a little too loudly.

"Think so. Reckon I got them varmints on the run. The trick'll be to get Lily Langtry back without any harm coming to her." Slocum saw only distress on the woman's pale face now.

"On the run?" Catherine repeated in a dull voice.

"They're hightailing it north, heading for El Paso or maybe even across the border into Mexico," he said, not sure where Utah and his partners might go. Lily had said they were from around Abilene, so it made sense they would go home. But he had told Bean he was crossing the Rio Grande. If Catherine ever mentioned any of this to the judge, Slocum wanted to be covered.

Most of all, he wanted to stir things up with the conniving Catherine Brookline.

"You needin' anything, Mr. Slocum? I heard tell you're ridin' for the judge," the stable owner called.

"Thanks, no. I've got all I need to bring in those sons of

bitches—or their heads, which is all the judge wants." Slocum tipped his hat in Catherine's direction and turned his horse's face, heading north toward Losier Canyon.

He felt good about his stay in Langtry. Damned good. Now it was time to bring everything together.

Slocum rode to the top of the rise and shielded his eyes, scanning the terrain behind him. He could not be certain but thought he saw dust clouds rising along the trail he had just traveled. He waited a few minutes, but the dust died down. He might have been wrong.

But he didn't think so.

Urging his horse back down the gentle slope, he avoided several thickets of prickly pear cactus. Slocum looked around, got his bearings and then went to the edge of the patch. He dug like a dog burying a bone for a few minutes, the hard, sun-baked dirt flying until he had a foot-deep hole. He dropped in the bag of silver Roy Bean had given him, covering it and dropping a couple dead prickly pear pads over the fresh dirt.

He brushed off the grit and again checked his bearings. He wanted to locate the hoard after he had recovered his brother's watch.

Slocum rode on, reaching Utah's camp just after twilight. The man jumped, as did his two companions. They had not bothered posting a guard.

"Where's Lily?" Slocum asked, swinging out of the saddle. He had ridden hard all day and was glad to be on solid ground again. His horse was also glad that Slocum was finally on solid ground again.

"She off in the bushes," Utah said. Slocum studied him and wondered if his name was Frank Dupree. Could be.

"I've got some news to pass along, and I don't want to say it twice. Go get her, will you, Dupree?" Slocum asked, watching to see what would happen. Utah took a step, then pivoted, facing Slocum.

"How'd you know my name?"

"Get Lily," Slocum said, keeping from smiling. He had them all eating out of his hand.

Utah—Frank Dupree—hurried off, calling to the woman. In a few minutes, the bushes rustled and Lily came out, smoothing her tattered skirts. She saw Slocum, waved and came to him.

"John, you made good time." She put her hand on his arm, but he did not respond. Slocum was past wanting anything to do with these people, save where it helped his cause.

"Gather round," Slocum said. He sat on one man's bed-roll and accepted a cup of coffee. From its bitter taste it had probably been boiled that morning. He wet his whistle, got some of the trail dust off his lips and then launched into his tall tale.

"You all are in big trouble. Judge Roy Bean's not going along with letting me handle this."

"But didn't you tell him you'd contacted the kidnappers?" asked Lily.

"Of course I did. He wanted you back then and there. Since you weren't riding along with me, he boiled over. Ranted and raved about stringing up everyone." Slocum paused for effect and then said, "He's sending out a big posse. He knew I'd come this way, so he reckoned this was where you were camped."

"We gotta get out of here!" cried Utah.

"Hold your horses. Sure you do, but if they find the camp deserted, they'll keep looking. If it looks as if you were attacked, that might throw them off the trail."

"Who'd attack us, other than Bean's posse?"

Slocum shrugged. "Bandidos, other outlaws. Might be some other posse out hunting you down. The judge's reward is a mighty handsome one. How long would it take you to earn two thousand dollars punching cows?"

"This ain't workin' out the way you said it would, Frank," complained one of the cowboys. "I'm clearin' out right now."

"Wait, wait," Slocum said. "We might work something out where we all ride on with a few dollars in our pockets."

"I don't care about the money," said the agitated cowboy. "I don't want to ride out and get a damn bullet in my back!"

"You won't," Slocum said, "if you don't panic. You can't stay here, that's for sure."

"John, what if I returned with you? Let Utah and the boys clear out." Lily moved closer to him. Slocum didn't push her away but felt like it. Her presence bothered him now, reminding him of what had been a moment of weakness. She was as much a con artist as Catherine. The two women had, after all, come west to bilk Roy Bean out of as much money as they could.

So far, only Catherine had profited by screwing every woman-hungry man in Langtry. Slocum counted on this to keep Lily on the hook. She wanted her cut of the money flowing out of that sleepy west Texas town.

"I can get rid of the posse. I'm sure of it. We can still collect the ransom. Bean won't let us near that reward without seeing some corpses." Slocum saw Utah and his two friends shudder. They knew of the judge's harsh justice and quick temper.

"So we—Utah and the boys and I—go somewhere else and let you argue with the judge's posse? That sounds dangerous," Lily said.

"For all of us," agreed Slocum. "It'll work. Go deeper into the canyon, find yourself a cave or somewhere along one wall where you can get water without going too far. Stick close to your camp until I come for you."

"What if the posse strings you up?" asked Utah. "I seen them boys when they get blood in their eyes. Friends turn to killers just like that." He snapped his fingers.

"I got to do something to earn my share," Slocum said, looking grim. He fought to keep from laughing at the way the men were scared. Lily's quick mind worked over ways of getting back to Langtry and collecting either the ransom or the reward for herself.

"Let's not tarry," Lily said, getting to her feet. "We don't know how far ahead of the posse John is."

"An hour or two, maybe. Time for you to find a new camp. Cover your trail real good," he added.

"How'll you find us? Should we tell you where we're heading?" asked Lily.

"No, don't do that. If the posse doesn't believe me, I don't want them torturing any information out of me," Slocum said. "What I don't know, I can't tell."

Utah tossed his head in Lily's direction, getting her moving. She hesitated and then came back and threw her arms around Slocum's neck, kissing him hard.

"Be careful, John," she whispered. "I want you back in one piece." She brushed her hand over his crotch in silent promise and then rushed off to climb onto the swaybacked horse that had been peacefully standing at the edge of the camp.

"Leave everything," Slocum said to Utah. "I'll take care of it. Don't worry about riding through camp and kicking up a ruckus. Make it look like a big posse has already been here."

He watched as Utah and the others rode back and forth through the camp and then headed due west. He figured they would turn and eventually go north, deeper into the canyon. Finding them would be the work of an hour or so, since Utah wasn't that good at hiding his tracks.

Slocum mounted his horse and forced it to go through the campfire a few times, scattering ash and ember so they would cool quickly. He crisscrossed the campsite several more times, making it appear as though a dozen or more men had hurrahed those around the fire. Then he went to a small stand of pinon not far away and tethered his horse. He broke out some of the supplies Bean had given him and ate a cold dinner.

Slocum settled down and waited, wondering if he had really seen riders following him. He had ridden like the wind, and they would have been tracking him, making them come along slower. Slocum drifted off to sleep and then came awake with a start a little before midnight.

The sound of horses caused him to reach for his six-shooter, but then he relaxed when he saw it wasn't a posse but only two riders.

"What happened?" came Catherine's startled voice. "They were supposed to be here, waiting for me!"

"How the hell can you drag her back if she's not where she's supposed to be?" groused the man with her. "And how the hell can we kill those sons o' bitches to collect the full reward?"

"Shut up, Davy," Catherine said sharply.

Slocum peered through the darkness and finally got a decent view of the man with her. He still wore the dirty overalls he had donned when he had gotten off the noonday train and had refilled the locomotive boiler with water. Davy had acted well, and Slocum had never known it was Catherine's brother getting off the train.

The mysterious telegram message now became clear. Catherine had telegraphed her brother to come on the noon train to Langtry from Del Rio. Why he had not died in the Mississippi was something Slocum didn't question—he simply accepted it as another piece of a dangerous puzzle.

"I want that money!" shouted the man, jerking the reins on his horse and turning it in a tight circle that kicked up dust from the abandoned camp.

"We don't have anything without the woman," Catherine said.

"This is a stupid idea you had, Catherine. I should never have let you talk me into it." Davy Brookline slapped his hand against his thigh, creating a sound like a gunshot.

"*Talk* you into it?" she scoffed. "After that gang of cutthroats tried to kill you in New Orleans, there was nothing you wouldn't have agreed to. You were flat broke and on the run. Should I let Yellow Henry know where you are? Do you think he'd come out here personally to rip you apart with his bare hands after what you did to him and the Spiders?"

The two continued to argue, affording Slocum some measure of enjoyment. By having Lily and the others move camp, he had denied Catherine the chance to murder the men and cart Lily back to her namesake town for the sizable reward. Slocum wondered if Lily was venal enough to go along with such a scheme and then decided he didn't want to know if she would murder her friends.

That Catherine thought it was a good idea was enough to cement his opinion of her. If he crossed her, he would be killed in a flash. Slocum vowed to cover his back at every turn.

"Split up," Davy said. "I'll go after them, and you return to Langtry and appease that old fool."

"Can you handle three men?" asked Catherine.

"They won't know what happened, but I have to find them first. If some other posse's after them, there's no way I can take on that many men."

Davy Brookline rode off in the wrong direction from camp and made far too much noise to ever hope of sneaking up on anyone not deaf or dead. Slocum had no worry that he would ever find Lily, Utah and the others, except by blind luck. He was a denizen of the city, not the country, and displayed poor trail instinct and knowledge. Slocum considered letting Davy thrash around and then putting a slug into him, but he was more interested in Catherine.

The woman dismounted and walked around the camp, as if she was reading what had really happened. A few times she kicked at burned wood or scorched rock from the campfire, as if trying to figure out how it all fit together. She finally shook her head, looked up at the nighttime sky and then mounted. She circled the camp one final time, coming within a few yards of where Slocum stood in shadow, watching her intently. Catherine never saw him and rode on, retracing her trail.

Slocum stared into the dark where Davy had gone and

then at Catherine's vanishing outline. The more interesting times would be in Langtry. Slocum took his time packing his supplies, mounted and set off after the woman, not hurrying to get to Langtry.

17

Slocum rested his horse frequently and didn't get into Langtry until well after sunrise began burning the west Texas town into submission. The day's heat was already starting to wear on him, and the horse needed watering something fierce, but the final stretch lured him on. Slocum dismounted and walked the struggling paint the rest of the way into town once he reached the outskirts of Langtry. As before, he felt eyes following every movement he made, eyes hidden behind buildings or inside in the dimness where it was still cool.

Before, he had been edgy. Now he felt downright good about returning to Langtry.

"Hey, Slocum, you got good news for the judge?" called a deputy, sitting with his feet up on a rail in front of the hoosegow and picking his teeth with a long, slender knife blade. "You don't, he might swing you jist for the hell of it." The deputy tossed the knife so it stuck, quivering, in a wood post holding up a shaky roof over the boardwalk where he sat.

The deputy laughed at this little joke.

Slocum didn't bother answering. He went directly to the stable and saw that his horse got tended to before he moseyed over to the Jersey Lily. Roy Bean had yet to bring his first defendant to trial, so the place was quiet.

Quiet, save for the way Catherine Brookline pleaded emotionally with the judge.

"Pay the ransom, Judge. You're the only one who can save her. Those are desperate men. They'll kill Mrs. Langtry." Catherine clutched one of the judge's gnarly hands in hers, bringing it to her breast in a dramatic gesture.

"Not one red cent fer ransom. I might jist make the reward *three* thousand dollars, though." Roy Bean looked up and saw Slocum standing in the door of the Jersey Lily. He bellowed at him, "Git yerself in here and let me know what's been goin' on, Slocum. I ain't outfittin' you to take a vacation at my expense."

"Haven't been lollygagging, Judge," Slocum said. He glanced in Catherine's direction. The woman's eyes narrowed, as if she suspected him of being her mortal enemy. That wasn't far from the truth, Slocum realized, but she held no fear of him because she didn't know yet that he had learned her brother was still alive.

That would come later.

"Chased 'em to the river, but there's a flood going on out there, in case you hadn't noticed. There's no way I can cross the Rio Grande until it goes down."

"Flood? In the middle of summer? Where's water like that comin' from?" asked Bean. "Never seen that 'fore now. Hell, it's been three months since we had so much as a rain cloud in the sky, much less real honest-to-God rain. My crossing's not got enough water to drown a flea."

"What's all this talk about water in the river?" asked Catherine. "Getting Mrs. Langtry back is what matters. Please, Judge, I beseech you! Pay the ransom and get Lily back safe and sound!"

Slocum heard the touch of hysteria in Catherine's voice. She didn't know what Slocum had been up to but wanted to secure the ransom money for herself. Once it was in her hands, she and Davy would likely light out and never be seen again. Even as that crossed his mind, Catherine outlined her bogus plan.

"I can get it to the kidnappers and guarantee her safe return. Trust me, Judge. I don't want a hair on that darling woman's head harmed."

"You mean you'd broker the exchange of money fer Mrs. Langtry? That's a dangerous spot to sit, Miss Brookline. Thems dangerous criminals, any buzzard what'd steal away a songbird of such refined looks and talent."

"For Mrs. Langtry, I'll do it," Catherine said earnestly.

"How are you going to cross the river?" Slocum asked, keeping up his end of the charade. "Those Mexican bandidos are not going to come back with her as long as they are safe in their own country. No posse can get to them."

"Mexicans? They don't have her," Catherine blurted.

"Who does, Miss Brookline?" asked Bean in a low voice that carried a considerable threat in it.

"I'll get you proof, Judge Bean. When I get back with it, you'll know I can save Lily!" With that Catherine stormed out, extricating herself from an argument that turned against her minute by minute.

"So, Slocum, gimme the details. Don't leave out a single one," warned Roy Bean.

Slocum smiled crookedly and said, "I got some facts in this case that'll curl your hair, Judge. Give me a few minutes, and a shot of that rotgut you call whiskey, and I'll tell you how everything can work itself out just fine."

It took Slocum an hour and half a bottle of trade whiskey before he got it all straight in Judge Roy Bean's mind.

It was nearly sunset when Slocum moved closer to the thick-walled adobe house where Catherine stayed. He listened hard for voices but heard nothing. The lathered horse tethered out back told him that Davy had returned from his futile search for Lily, Utah and the others, and he wanted to know more.

Slocum edged around until he came to the front. The

door stood ajar to let in some of the weak evening breeze. He sank down, his back against the still-warm adobe, as Catherine and Davy started arguing again. He wondered if that was all this brother and sister did.

"Nothing! What do you mean you found nothing! They're out there! Slocum knows where they are!"

"He's bluffing. He's working some kind of snake oil game on that old buzzard of a judge. I tell you, they ran like rabbits and didn't even leave behind a pellet or two as they went."

"Davy, Davy, are you an idiot? I know her. She's not going to give up on getting *some* of the money, either reward or ransom."

"You don't know her, Sis," said Davy Brookline. "She's just some dance hall tart you hired in New Orleans."

"I know the type, Davy," Catherine said acidly. "If she smells a greenback, she'll come running."

"I can hunt for them again, but it's not going to amount to anything," Davy said, turning sullen.

"Always giving up. You never stick to anything, do you?" accused his sister. "If they were all dead, I could get the ransom money. I have Lily's trunk with all her costumes in it. A piece of ribbon, some sign she was still alive and Bean would pony up the money so fast it'd make our heads spin."

"You're a good actress, sis. Why don't you dress up and pretend you're Lily Langtry? We could set it up so he wouldn't see you up close, just enough to pay the ransom. You could ride around out in the twilight so's he could see the clothes and let you call out to him, 'Help me, Judge, help me.' Then you could ride off a ways out of sight and get rid of the clothes and make it look as if Lily lit out. We'd have the money, and he'd think Lily had double-crossed him or maybe the kidnappers had snatched her away again."

Slocum wondered if Davy and Catherine lay awake nights thinking up such complicated schemes to bilk others of their money or if it just came naturally to them.

"Too chancy. Besides, I've offered to be the courier for the money. How could I both carry the money and show myself as Lily?"

Catherine's objection was a good one, but Slocum read more into it. She had to be given the money because she wanted to deal her brother out of this hand, too. A full thousand dollars in ransom was a prettier sight than just half.

The two kept arguing and scheming. Slocum tired of spying on them and slipped back around the adobe until he got to his own horse. It was dark along the road out of Langtry, but Slocum had ridden it enough times to know every rock and pothole. Moreover, he saw no reason to hurry. Let Catherine and Davy hatch another plot.

All that mattered was Judge Roy Bean seeing his inamorata Lily Langtry and handing over the money for her safe return.

Slocum awoke just after dawn, having camped deep in Losier Canyon. He had ignored the old campsite where Utah had fled. Following the trail, even knowing the direction taken, would have been impossible in the moonless night, so Slocum had decided to catch up on some much-needed sleep. He stretched, yawned and fixed himself a generous portion of food for breakfast. Only when he was feeling fit enough to tangle with a wildcat did he begin tracking.

Utah had done a passable job hiding his tracks, but Slocum was as good a tracker as any Apache. Long years seeing every trick played—and thinking up a few of his own—stood him in good stead. A little after high noon he rode into Utah's camp.

Slocum shook his head as he entered. Nobody stood sentry. Utah was either the stupidest man on the face of the planet or else he had a trusting soul. Not believing Utah had much in the way of a soul left Slocum with only one conclusion.

"John! You're back!" cried Lily. She came running up from the direction of a stream, her hair wet and her clothing clinging damply to her body. She had been bathing. Slocum reckoned this was where Utah and the other two had been, also.

Not bathing, but spying on Lily as she cleaned some of the dust off her luscious body.

He dismounted as Utah and his partners came out of the nearby stand of pines, looking sheepish. Slocum's guess about what they had been doing was right on target, but he said nothing. The chance of Davy finding them was slim, and Roy Bean had not sent out the posse Slocum had feared he might. For the reward money, though, men might be scattered across half of west Texas hunting for Lily.

"What's happening?" Lily demanded, clinging to Slocum's arm.

"What do you know about Catherine Brookline?" he asked.

Utah and the others exchanged glances and then suspiciously looked at Lily. She tried to seem nonchalant.

"Not much. She approached me because she liked my performance. I had seen her and her brother a few times before, over the years. She had been quite an attraction a few years ago but for some reason she left the stage."

"Setting up fake kidnappings probably turned out to be more profitable," Slocum said sarcastically. "Double-crossing the people involved also seems a way for Catherine to make a few extra dollars."

"What are you saying? Is she leading the posse to us?" Utah's hand went to his six-shooter, but he did not draw. For all the appearance of a gunman, Utah lacked the moves. Slocum doubted he could even shoot straight.

"Her brother's not dead, as I'd thought," Slocum said. "He's scouring the territory for you, intending to kill you all and take Lily back."

"I'd tell Roy!" Lily exclaimed.

Slocum wondered at her loyalty to Utah but said nothing about that. He had a different argument.

"If you could even talk. Wouldn't it be terrible if the kidnappers cut out your tongue? Or beat you so severely you were in a coma? Bean said he wanted you back safe and sound, but if Davy claims he found you in that condition—and brings the heads of the men responsible—I don't think the judge is going to dig too hard to find the truth."

"That's terrible!" cried Lily, her hand going to her throat. "How could they do such a thing!"

"You fell in with dangerous friends," Slocum pointed out.

"No friend of mine would do that!" protested Lily. She settled down a mite and asked Slocum, "What are we going to do? Just leave? There's that lovely money, but if it means Utah and the others might be harmed, why, I'd give it up in a flash!"

Her words said one thing, but the cold calculation going on in her mind said another. Slocum read it in her eyes and the way she sat. Lily would abandon Utah if she had any chance at waltzing away with the ransom money.

Slocum sat back as Utah, Lily and the others argued over what they ought to do. He remembered how Davy and Catherine had fought the same way over the same matter. Getting Judge Roy Bean's money was all that was on their minds. He had not fallen in with one den of thieves but two. Then he smiled. Judge Bean and all his scheming was hardly as pure as the wind-driven virgin snow. Three sets of thieves, each angling to do the other out of money.

Of the lot, only Roy Bean showed an ounce of human decency in the matter, though. He was willing to pay to get Lily back, but not if it was ransom money. Any amount for a reward, but nothing for ransom.

Slocum thought that might change, should he bring the judge sufficient proof that Lily was still alive.

"If you're all done bickering," Slocum said, "let me tell

you how we might all come out of this sewer smelling like roses."

He found it far easier convincing this pack of thieves what they ought to do than he thought. Dangle a few dollars and they would agree to anything.

They broke camp in the morning, and Slocum continued along the road back to Langtry, hoping it would be for the last time.

18

The entire town was abuzz. Slocum felt the renewed energy and maybe, just maybe, the lessening of fear gripping it other times he had been here. That meant Judge Roy Bean had come to a conclusion about Mrs. Lily Langtry and her kidnappers' ransom demand. Slocum sucked in his breath and held it. There was a good chance Catherine had convinced the judge she ought to act as intermediary in the exchange and that Slocum knew nothing about Lily's whereabouts.

If so, Slocum might find himself in a world of trouble. The only way to find out was to ask Roy Bean.

"You look to be ridin' in empty-handed, Slocum," called the deputy who seemed to be a permanent fixture in front of the *juzgado*. The only change was in where he thrust his feet. He had dropped them from the rail to the boardwalk.

"What's all the activity in town over?" Slocum asked.

"Things are poppin'. Lot of sightings of Mrs. Langtry— and none of 'em have a danged thing to do with you. You been across the river already?" The deputy laughed, telling Slocum more than he had known before. And it might not be so good for him.

He dismounted, whipped the reins around a hitching post and went into the Jersey Lily, where Bean already held court. The man was dispensing justice with his usual steely gaze and ornery disposition. Slocum's fingers twitched slightly, and he thought how easy it would be to gun down the judge. Even with two deputies in the saloon, he could pump a round or two into the judge for all he had done.

But the watch would be lost, even if Slocum managed to get away scot-free.

"There you be, Slocum. Git on over here and tell me what you found. You couldn't have got across the Rio Grande, not and be back this fast."

"You're right, Judge. I shouted across to one of the bandidos and—"

"He's lying, Judge. He wants to steal the money." Catherine looked as if she would explode in anger at any moment. Slocum guessed she had not done well convincing Bean to trust her.

"Oh, I don't think Slocum'd do a thing like that," chuckled Bean. "He wants something more 'n money, more 'n life. I seen the way he looked at me when he came into the courtroom." Bean sniffed the shot of whiskey he had sitting at his right, knocked back the shot and waited for Charlie to refill the glass. "He's not goin' nowhere 'til I say, are you, Slocum?"

"What's she got to offer she hasn't before?" Slocum asked. He stared coldly at Catherine, challenging her. "I know where Mrs. Langtry is."

"So do I!" cried Catherine. "Slocum's done nothing to get her back. Empty words, nothing more. Look, look what I have!" Catherine pulled out a dirty scarf. "She wore this when she was kidnapped. I have it as a measure of faith she's unharmed."

"The bandidos have her, and she wasn't wearing that scarf when she was taken, Judge," Slocum said. "Catherine took it from Mrs. Langtry's costume trunk." He remembered how Catherine and Davy had plotted this. He had hoped they would come up with something more interesting to sway Bean.

"These Mexicans," Catherine said, seeing Bean was buying it, "are dangerous men, but they are not stupid. They want the ransom money. And their patience is running out. They'll do something none of us want if you don't pay up quick."

"She's right on that score, Judge," Slocum said. "They got across the river somehow, and they can get back. It's not likely they'll take Lily with them if they go. Putting a reward on their heads won't matter if she's dead and they are in Mexico, beyond your reach."

Judge Roy Bean stroked his gray-flecked beard and was deep in thought. "I been reconsiderin' that. My temper mighta got the best of me. When I thought it was American kidnappers, well, that was one thing. Lettin' 'em escape across the border if they kill her ain't somethin' I cotton to very much."

"You'll pay the ransom?" asked Catherine, her eyes glowing with triumph.

"Reckon you talked me into it. None of the folks out scourin' the countryside has come up with squat, 'cept you two. I thought somebody'd have her back by now."

"They won't deal with her, Judge," Slocum spoke up. "They are Mexicans. Bandits of the worst kind. They don't respect women. They would kidnap Catherine, too, take the money and there'd be no telling what they might do to her *and* Mrs. Langtry."

Catherine shot him a look of pure venom.

"I'm no fool. I can deal with them."

"A fast gun is needed more than a fast word," Slocum cut in.

"A fast gun's likely to get Lily killed," Catherine said hotly.

"I agree with her, Slocum," Bean said. "You done had yer chance. She knows Mrs. Langtry, and she can spout them purty words. Mexicans, even Mexican bandidos, like that."

"You won't regret it, Judge Bean," Catherine said, putting her hands on his. He moved away so he could drink another shot of his potent firewater. From the strong odor, Slocum guessed the judge had been drinking heavily since Mrs. Langtry had been abducted. That might be clouding his reason now.

Slocum hoped not.

"Miss Brookline, I'll get you the money. I got tons of it, anyway, and what good's any of it do if a fine lady like Mrs. Langtry comes to harm?"

"Lots?" asked Catherine, her brilliant blue eyes now dancing with greed.

"I got a whole damn strongbox crammed full of gold and silver. Then there's another two boxes with nothing but scrip. I don't like greenbacks much, but sometimes a man's gotta take what he can from deadbeat convicts. So many pay their fines in it, I'm thinkin' of doublin' any levied fee paid for in foldin' money."

"Let's get it, Judge. I want to be on the trail as quickly as possible." Catherine rubbed her hands up and down the sides of her skirt, but she always hesitated when she came to a certain spot that seemed heavier than the rest of the fabric. Slocum wondered if she had a derringer hidden there.

"I'm so filthy rich I wonder why I stay out here, other 'n I love the people and the country so much," Bean went on. He took another drink of whiskey, then choked. Charlie slapped him hard on the back. It didn't help.

"Judge, what's wrong?" cried the barkeep. Charlie kept pounding, but Roy Bean sagged forward like a bag of doorknobs. His face turned fiery red, and he gasped for breath.

"Cain't breathe. And pain. Lordy, I got pain all over my chest."

"Heart attack," Slocum muttered. Catherine turned to him, horror on her face.

"No!" she gasped. The dark-haired woman spun about and reached over the plank bar that served as the judge's bench. She put her hands on either side of his head, holding it firmly. "Tell me you're all right, Judge Bean!"

"So near to seein' my angel, Mrs. Langtry ag'in," gasped Bean. "Lemme see her one more time 'fore I die." He coughed and gasped and crashed to the floor, slipping out of Catherine's feverish grasp.

"Get the doctor!" Slocum snapped at a deputy who was standing and staring. The man gaped until Slocum shoved him toward the door of the Jersey Lily.

"He can't die. All that money. Where is it, Judge? Tell me where the money is so I can rescue Lily!" pleaded Catherine.

"Where nobody'll ever find it," Bean said through clenched teeth. "World's gettin' kinda dark all around. Where are you, my darlin' Mrs. Langtry? Where?"

The door to the saloon slammed back and a tall, cadaverous man rushed in and knelt beside the judge. He fumbled to open his small bag.

"He'll be all right, won't he, Doctor?" asked Catherine.

The man looked up and smiled lugubriously. He shook his head. "I'm not the doc. I'm the town undertaker." He took a tape measure from his back and measured the judge's length. The man looked up and said almost apologetically, "Coffin's got to be a mite wider 'n I usually make. Length is fine, but the width?" He mumbled to himself as he measured Bean's girth.

"Get the hell out of my way, you soul-stealing jackass!" barked a stout man carrying a bag similar to the undertaker's. "I *am* the doctor in these parts, and you won't be takin' my patient any sooner than necessary." He pushed the undertaker away and began rummaging in his bag. Smelling salts waving back and forth under the judge's nose caused him to twitch and thrash about.

"Mrs. Langtry," Bean called weakly. "I'll give anything, ever'thing, to whoever brings the darling lady back to me 'fore I go on to the Promised Land."

"Everything, Judge?" Catherine asked.

The judge nodded weakly.

"Get out of here. Can't you see the man's sick? I need to get him to bed where he can rest. You, you, help me!" The doctor got Bean onto the same plank he had used as his judicial bench, and four men struggled to get him out of the Jersey Lily and around back to his office.

"What are we going to do?" Catherine said, stunned at the sudden rush of events. "We get that whore back and he'll pay. Nothing's likely to persuade him to tell us where he's hid his money."

"We?" asked Slocum. "How come you're dealing me into this hand, Catherine?"

"You're the only one who knows where she is, that's why," raged Catherine. "You and her and that idiot cowboy boyfriend of hers—"

"Utah?"

"Him. You're all in cahoots," she said hotly. "We can work together and get *something* out of this mess."

"Why should I bother?" he asked. "I can bring her back . . ." Slocum's voice trailed off.

"What's wrong?" asked Catherine.

"I wasn't lying about the Mexican bandidos. They didn't kidnap her, but they've got Lily. They killed Utah and the others with him. I found the camp, and the bandidos had overrun it. They may have heard about the reward, but they knew Bean would never believe they hadn't kidnapped her themselves."

"You're joking." Catherine was aghast. Slocum shook his head and looked solemn.

"I need the ransom if I'm going to get her back."

"A thousand dollars? Only Bean has that kind of money."

"I might dicker with them and get her back for less. They're mighty scared of him. More 'n that, they might want to please him, if a little money came their way. Roy Bean has quite a reputation, and they can't know he's had a heart attack."

"How much do you have?" Catherine stared at him, her mind working hard.

"Not much. A few of those greenbacks Bean despises so." Slocum pulled out a sweat-stained roll of scrip and counted through it. "Thirty-two dollars isn't enough. I'm not sure I can shoot it out with them all by myself. If I brought a posse, I'd never get within a mile of them before they hightailed it across the Rio Grande."

"What are we going to do?" Catherine was beside herself now. She started pacing, her eyes fixed on the sawdust-covered saloon floor.

"You got any money? Anything to prime the pump? I might dangle a few dollars in front of them, promising more later."

"I've got almost a thousand," Catherine said, then bit her lip as if she had spoken out of turn. Slocum said nothing and let the woman stew in her own juices. "I got it from the men in this flea-bitten town. Oh, hell, I'll get it and you get her back. We can get the *entire* poke Bean has salted away."

"Lily's going to be relieved to be saved," Slocum said. "She'll go along with about anything."

"Just be sure she keeps that filthy mouth of hers closed. If she says the wrong thing, Bean's likely to string up the lot of us."

Slocum took a drink of the whiskey Roy Bean had been swilling. He made a face. The cactus juice was worse than usual. Slocum sat heavily at a nearby table and waited for Catherine. He wondered what was in store for her. He knew how his side of the charade would play out, but Catherine— and Davy—had a way of playing wild cards when he least expected it.

He remembered Davy taking his dive face-first into the Mississippi. Slocum would have bet anything the man had died then and there.

Slocum perked up when Catherine hurried back, clutching a small leather bag. She tossed it onto the table.

"Don't open it," she cautioned. "Flashing that much money will only cause folks to wonder."

Slocum squeezed the bag and heard the crinkling of greenbacks inside. He took a deep breath, then tucked the bag into his gun belt. He longed for another drink but wanted to keep a clear head for what was going to happen.

"I'll be back as quick as I can. It's going to work out just fine, Catherine," he told her. "We'll get all of Bean's money in return for Lily."

"When he shows us the stash, we can kill him and take it all and be out of here before any of those fool deputies know anything's wrong. We can always say Bean died of another heart attack. What'll they know?" said Catherine, still scheming.

"We might not have to go that far. He might actually die of a heart attack and save us the trouble," Slocum said. "First, I have to fetch Lily from those murdering bandidos."

"Lily Langtry," scoffed the dark-haired beauty. She sneered, and her beauty vanished. "I should have slit her throat back in Fort Worth."

"There'll be time for all that later," Slocum assured her. He quickly left, mounted his horse and rode out of Langtry.

Slocum rode at a brisk clip, watchful of anyone on his trail. He wasn't too surprised when a lone horseman picked up his tracks and followed him a mile or so back. Slocum kept up the pace, putting ever more distance between himself and the man following him.

When Slocum reached the clump of prickly pears where he had buried Bean's five hundred dollars in silver, he jumped down and dug furiously, like a dog hunting for a bone. He found the silver and added to it the bag Catherine had given him. Slocum hesitated, then opened the bag, just to be sure.

A smile blossomed on his dusty face. Greenbacks—and lots of them. She hadn't tried cheating him. He doubted this was anywhere near the full amount she had bilked from the citizens of Langtry, but it was enough to keep Slocum happy. He hastily pushed the dirt back over the hoard and got back in the saddle, riding more slowly now to allow his tracker to catch up.

The chill of the desert night began gripping the land, and Slocum shivered slightly. Then he realized it was not so much the cold as the sensation of having someone sighting along a rifle barrel at his spine. He turned in the saddle and looked back along the trail.

Nothing.

The feeling of being watched intensified. He rode on, doubling back once but finding no one. The man chasing him all the way from Langtry had vanished. That put him on edge. It had not been coincidence that the man was tearing along after him any more than it was the man had vanished.

Slocum dismounted and found a secluded spot to sit and wait. He wanted a fire but knew the smoke and glare would draw more than insects. After a spell, he got hungry and stood to paw through the generous supplies still in his saddlebags.

The click of a round chambering in a rifle warned him. He flung himself to one side as the rifle spat leaden death in his direction. Slocum hit the ground hard, rolled and came to a sitting position, his Colt Navy out and ready to fire.

But where? Darkness all around masked his attacker. When the foot-long orange flame stabbed from the top of a boulder, Slocum knew where his ambusher lay. He returned fire, but neither of them came close to hitting their targets.

Silence descended, an eerie silence that worried Slocum.

Then another bullet whistled through the air, took off Slocum's hat and sent him staggering backward. He fell heavily to the ground and lay there unmoving.

Davy Brookline came down from the rocks, wary of a trap. He moved closer and kicked Slocum in the ribs. No movement. No breath, nothing.

"Good riddance, you stupid son of a bitch," Davy growled. He dropped to his knees and searched Slocum, ripping open pockets. He found the small roll of greenbacks and stuffed it into his own pocket, but he kept hunting.

"Where'd you put the money you got from Catherine?" Davy said, his anger mounting. He rolled Slocum over and searched his back pockets. Nothing. Then he left him on the ground and went to Slocum's horse. Ten minutes of hunting failed to gain him any of the money.

"You no-good son-of-a-*bitch*!" Davy shrieked. His anger knew no bounds. He cocked his rifle and pointed it at Slocum's dark form on the ground. Firing, he laughed in glee at taking some measure of revenge.

Then Davy heard shouts from up in the canyon.

"*¡Vamanos, muchachos! ¡Arriba!*"

Davy cussed a blue streak and ran for his horse, getting into the saddle and heading back in the direction of Langtry before the Mexican bandidos caught him.

19

"Is he dead?" came a curious voice.

"He can't be!" a woman cried. Slocum felt his head being lifted. A million ants dug around inside his brain, but he was aware of Lily cradling his head in her lap. He opened his eyes and saw her staring down at him and knew he wasn't dead.

Lily wouldn't be in heaven.

"Creased me," Slocum muttered from between dried lips. He struggled to sit up but was too dizzy. Lily held him close while Utah got a canteen and dribbled water onto his lips until he felt better. When he did get to his feet, he was weak and wobbly but alive.

"You let him shoot you to make him think he'd killed you," marveled Lily. "How brave a man you are!"

Slocum winced as he moved. A pain in the middle of his back refused to go away. He twisted and felt the sharp splinter of rock in his back. In the dark, Davy had fired but had missed, hitting a rock that sent a fragment into Slocum's back. The blood from this tiny wound had convinced the man his second bullet had robbed his victim of his life.

"What was that sidewinder huntin' for?" asked Utah. "We rode up 'bout the time he was rummagin' through your saddlebags."

"Food, probably," Slocum lied.

"You know him?" asked Utah.

Slocum didn't answer directly. He looked at Lily to see if she had recognized Catherine's brother. Slocum realized she might never have seen Davy Brookline back in New Orleans.

"That was Catherine's brother," Slocum said slowly. "They're trying to bamboozle Judge Bean into thinking you are dead so they can swindle him out of the ransom money."

"Cut me out, will they!" raged Lily. She stamped her foot and crossed her arms over her breasts. "We got here in time, Utah. If this Davy Brookline had killed Slocum, we'd have never known who shot him or why."

"That was real smart shouting out in Spanish," Slocum said. Utah grinned and looked as if he would blush at the compliment.

"You told us to do that," Lily pointed out. "If we saw anyone coming, we were to shout something in Spanish. It's good that Utah knew some. The words I know are much less . . . genteel."

Slocum had to laugh. "That would have done just fine, Lily. He thought the Mexicans were hot after him, and that drove him back to Langtry."

"What do we do now, John?" the woman asked.

"Why, I thought you would have figured that out by now." Slocum told them, although it took him some time to properly convince them he knew what he was doing.

"The town doesn't look any different," Lily said as they rode into Langtry the next afternoon. "I reckon it'll never look much different, will it?"

"No," was all Slocum said. Most of the townsfolk were indoors sleeping through the heat. He had planned it so they would return when they were least likely to be seen. All Bean's deputies would be taking their siestas, too, so they could ride directly for the office behind the Jersey Lily.

"What's the occasion?" Utah asked nervously, pointing to the horses and buggies around the small adobe office where the doctor had taken Roy Bean after his heart attack.

"Let's find out." Slocum had to reassure Utah there wasn't any trouble brewing.

Slocum knocked on the door and went inside when Bean growled. The judge lay on a cot on the far side of the room. With him were the doctor, his barkeep and a couple others Slocum recognized as being the closest thing Langtry had to town fathers.

"Mrs. Langtry!" shouted Bean, rocketing off the cot so fast it turned over. He was dressed in his union suit and nothing more. He stopped and looked down and seemed almost embarrassed for a lady to see him like this. He said sheepishly, "I wasn't expectin' company, much less your loveliness."

"Always the gentleman, Judge," Lily said graciously. "After all I've been through, seeing you at all is a sight for sore eyes."

"What about these varmints?" asked Bean, squinting at Utah and the other two. "Ain't they the ones who kidnapped you?"

"No!" spoke up Slocum. "They helped me rescue Mrs. Langtry from the Mexican bandidos. They're cowpokes from up Abilene way. This here's Frank Dupree and—" Slocum had never heard the others' names.

"Jess Westcott," said one in a thin voice. The other croaked out, "My handle's Tex Murch."

"So they rescued her?" demanded Bean.

"They did," Slocum said firmly. "If it weren't for them, I'd never have gotten Mrs. Langtry away from those bandidos."

"Right," Bean said.

"Judge, Mr. Slocum is leaving out a vital part of the story, because he was sorely injured during my rescue. I know the leader of the Mexicans."

Slocum said nothing. They had rehearsed this all the way

into Langtry. It was time to pay back some of the Brook-lines' double-dealing.

"A man calling himself Davy was their leader. He was the mastermind of the kidnapping, and I don't think he is a Mexican. The bandidos are back across the border, but I suspect this Davy returned to Langtry."

"This here owlhoot's not goin' far," Bean announced. He spoke rapidly to the two men Slocum thought were local politicians. They hurried out, probably to tell the deputies.

Just then Catherine came in. "Judge, you're feeling bet-ter, I see. I was so worried. I—" She gasped and went deathly pale when she saw Slocum, Lily and the other three in the office.

"What's wrong, Catherine? Cat got your tongue?" Lily asked with some venom. "Judge Bean, bless his generous soul, was just getting ready to pay out the reward to these brave men for rescuing me."

"But she, you—" Catherine gulped and stared at Slocum. "You're dead!" she blurted.

"As dead as I thought Davy was," Slocum said so low only she could hear.

"Judge Bean, how did you make such a speedy recov-ery?" Catherine asked, struggling to cover her panic. "You're looking positively wonderful!"

"Nothin' ever wrong with me. I was playactin', good enough to impress even a professional like Mrs. Langtry. It was a shame her kidnapper was the only one taken in by my performance."

Slocum felt sorry for Catherine, but only for a moment. He doubted she had sent Davy after him with the intent of dry-gulching him. Her brother had taken what he saw as a golden opportunity to steal his sister's share of the money off a dead enemy.

Catherine was being hoodwinked by her own flesh and blood.

"Judge," Catherine said. "Since Mrs. Langtry is back where she belongs, then I get the reward."

"No, little lady, that's not the way I see it," Bean said. "These gents get it. From what Mrs. Langtry tells me, I might as well divvy up the two thousand dollars betweenst them."

"That's most generous, Judge," Lily said, keeping Utah and the other two silent so they wouldn't muddy the waters.

"You never had a heart attack," Catherine said, looking from Bean to Slocum.

"Strong as a mule, that's me," Bean bragged. "Now if you ladies and gents will excuse me, I got to get dressed. When I finish, meet me in the Jersey Lily. I got some judging to do."

"Why, yes, yes, of course," Catherine said, backing out. She got to the office door, turned and ran.

In the hot sun again, Lily shielded her eyes with her hand as she watched Catherine sprinting for her house across Langtry's main street.

"She's going to turn into a jackrabbit. You think we should let her go, John, after all she's done?"

A million thoughts floated through Slocum's head, all fragmented and confused. Some were pleasant, others were not.

"Let her go. She's got enough sense to realize all her scheming hasn't worked out."

"You and the judge faked a heart attack?" Lily asked. "To throw Catherine off?"

"Something like that," Slocum said, wanting to change the topic. He had most of the dark-haired beauty's money buried with the silver Bean had given him. Supplies for another week rode in his saddlebags. If he could get out of town, he would be well paid for his trouble.

Slocum corrected himself. He had to leave *with* the watch.

"So you told Roy Bean everything?" asked Lily. "Everything?"

"Not that much," Slocum allowed. "Just what he needed to know about Catherine and Davy."

"What about us?" asked Utah.

"Take the money Bean gives you and get the hell out of town," advised Slocum.

"Hold your horses, boys," Lily said. "You try riding out with *my* share and you'll wish the buzzards had pecked out your eyes in the middle of the noonday desert!"

"I wouldn't cross you," Utah said.

"No, I don't think you would," Lily said, seeing what Slocum already had. Utah had a real crush on the woman.

They went into the saloon, and Slocum got a bottle of what looked to be the best liquor in the house. The tequila burned, but it was good feeling its potency pooling in his belly. Bean's trade whiskey had been giving him headaches. Slocum and the others had finished their first round and were working on a second when Bean came in, followed by his deputies. All of them were sweating hard.

"What was that ruckus outside a minute or two ago?" Lily asked.

"Some unfinished business. Nothin' to bother yerself over, my dear." Bean planted himself behind the bar and motioned for Charlie and a deputy to heave the plank back over the barrels used to support his "bench."

"You boys, come on over here," Bean said to Utah and his partners. Nervously they went to the bench of justice. To their relief Bean dropped a bag filled with gold onto the plank. "Your reward. A thousand dollars."

"You promised two, Judge," protested Slocum.

"Might be my mind got a little foggy from my 'heart attack,' Slocum," Bean said sternly. "You boys have any objections?"

"No, sir, none, not at all," babbled Utah. He scooped up the coins and backed off, as if he were in the presence of European royalty rather than a ragtag second-rate judge in a third-rate town.

"Good. Now where's Catherine Brookline?"

"She lit out, Judge," a deputy said. "You want us to run her down and drag her back?"

Roy Bean thought for a moment, looked at Slocum, then said, "Let the vixen go." He took a deep breath, reached out so Charlie could thrust a shot glass filled with whiskey into his hand, and then said, "That concludes judicial business. Let the party begin! Mrs. Lily Langtry is back in town!"

Slocum drank but looked for the chance to ask Bean for his watch. He had done everything he could and had even saved Lily's life—whatever her real name might be. Then Slocum decided it did not matter. For the evening, she *was* Lily Langtry, dancing with Roy Bean and singing badly and entertaining everyone in the town.

But the watch. He finally sidled over to the judge when he and Lily were tuckered out from yet another fast dance.

"Judge, I need to talk to you," Slocum said.

"And I want a word with you, Slocum. I telegraphed down to Del Rio and have a special train comin' break of dawn tomorrow to take Mrs. Langtry to San Antone."

"You want I should escort her?" Slocum asked.

"No need. Lily—Mrs. Langtry—thought since they had done such a fine job already, maybe them three cowboys that saved her from the bandidos might escort her."

"Reckon she'd be safe with them. They've proved themselves trustworthy."

"They have," Bean agreed, looking as Lily talked with Utah in guarded tones. "Be at the depot to see her off."

"Judge—"

"Not now, boy. It's time to finish this here shindig!" cried Judge Roy Bean. If Slocum had not worried so about the return of his watch, he would have said it was the grandest party he had ever attended.

Dawn was breaking when the locomotive chugged into the station. The stationmaster hurried out and waved feebly, as if the engineer would steam on past without his signal. Lily had her luggage piled up in a small mountain, waiting to be loaded on the train. Utah and his two partners stood around, whispering among themselves. Slocum figured Lily had already taken her share of the reward. Still, each man was $250 richer for his trouble. Slocum knew better than to ask for a cut of the reward. He had a few cuts and scrapes, had been duped and shot, but had come out better than Catherine Brookline.

The woman had known what awaited her in Langtry and had left town so fast she had not bothered to take her clothes with her.

Of her brother, Slocum had not seen hide nor hair.

"There it is, Mrs. Langtry," said Bean, stepping up and putting his arm around her slender waist. "Time for you to get on to San Antone for your performance."

Roy Bean held out a flyer. She stared at it. Slocum thought she was going to faint dead away. From where he stood, he saw the broadside had a remarkably clear picture of the real Jersey Lily on it.

"Go on, my dear. Amaze them with your voice and style and grace, jist like you did me and the rest of Langtry, Texas!"

"Thank you, Judge," Lily said in a small voice. She kissed him quickly, then rushed to the train. Utah and the other two struggled with her trunks and then boarded the lone passenger car with the woman.

Roy Bean waved as the special train chugged out of the station, on its way to San Antonio.

The judge heaved a deep sigh and said, "A fine lady. Yes, sir, Slocum, a grand lady."

Slocum wondered if the judge had not recognized the difference between the woman pictured on the flyer and the woman calling herself Lily Langtry.

Bean held up his hand to forestall any such question. "That picture did not do justice to a fine and lovely woman." Roy Bean smiled and added, "All a man really has in this sorry goddamn world are his private dreams." He fished in his vest pocket and drew out Slocum's watch. It spun slowly, catching golden rays of dawn breaking over west Texas. Judge Roy Bean handed it to Slocum, then went off whistling.

"I'll be damned," Slocum said.

He jumped down from the platform and went to get his paint horse and supplies from the livery. It was time to move on—to a certain patch of prickly pear cactus out Losier Canyon way, and the fifteen hundred dollars in greenbacks and silver coin buried there.

Slocum mounted and rode slowly from Langtry, now stirring before the heat squeezed life from it again. He wondered how Lily and Utah would do in San Antonio. He wished them only the best. And Catherine? What would become of her? Slocum didn't know and didn't care.

At the edge of town, Slocum reined back and stared at the telegraph pole. Swinging slowly, a noose tight around his neck, was Davy Brookline. He knew now what Bean's unfinished business had been the day before, right after Catherine had hightailed it but before Bean had given the reward to Utah and his partners. Once alerted, the judge's deputies had found Davy Brookline in a hurry.

Justice had come even faster.

Slocum put his spurs to his horse's flanks and trotted out of town, wanting to get away from Judge Roy Bean and his claim of being the Law West of the Pecos.

JAKE LOGAN
TODAY'S HOTTEST ACTION WESTERN!

J. R. ROBERTS
THE GUNSMITH